Changeling Press, LLC

ChangelingPress.com

Wolf Schooled

A Searchlight Paranormal Romance

Emily Carrington

Wolf Schooled
A Searchlight Paranormal Romance
Emily Carrington

All rights reserved.
Copyright ©2022 Emily Carrington

ISBN: 978-1-60521-812-0

Publisher:
Changeling Press LLC
315 N. Centre St.
Martinsburg, WV 25404
ChangelingPress.com

Printed in the U.S.A.

Editor: Crystal Esau
Cover Artist: Angela Knight

The individual stories in this anthology have been previously released in E-Book format.

Table of Contents

Midnight Sons (Wolf Schooled 1)
Emily Carrington

Amaruq is a *FTM* transgender werewolf. Though confident in his own body, he runs up against the challenges of living and loving in a college environment. These pale when compared to the violence he is subjected to.

Nootaikok is a former tracker, a killer who is looking for a new lease on life. He finds his solace in Amaruq. But when that way of life is threatened by terrorists, he must reclaim his former training, despite his demons, or see his love die.

Can Amaruq and Nootaikok's love rise from the ashes of disaster like the storied phoenix?

Chapter One

Amaruq's birth name was Mary.

Screw that. I've been Amaruq to my new werewolf pack since mid-summer. Even Tilthos Charles, the alpha above all alphas in North America, calls me Amaruq. I'm no more Mary than I am female.

But he was still biologically female, at least on the outside. Damn werewolves for not knowing how to perform gender reassignment surgery. And since humans -- most of them anyway -- didn't know werewolves, or any other magical creatures, existed, there would be no asking them for help.

Amaruq rolled his head to the right against the plane's hard seatback and closed his eyes. *Tilthos Charles calls me Amaruq. Which is a male name as well as my true name. Even if my parents call me Mary still, they're in Anchorage and I'm, well, I'm not technically in Buffalo or even the surrounding area.*

He glanced out the window at the brightness of the sky above the clouds. *I'm on my way to SearchLight Academy for my second semester. And, yeah, I'm Mary on their books, but my professors don't call me that after the first day, and my friends not since I introduced myself as Amaruq. SearchLight is much more accepting of transgender Inuit werewolves. Maybe once I have the money, I'll get my name legally changed.*

With this current bout of vitriol out of his spleen, and with a smile borne of that last idea, Amaruq fell asleep. He'd been up early, unable to sleep, and he needed a short nap. He dreamed of the short, ebony-haired Inuit shifter who had populated his dreams for some time. Being a precognitive, Amaruq had faith his dream would come true. He settled in mentally to enjoy its oft-repeated flow.

First, he found himself in a kayak in the middle of the Arctic Ocean. There were narwhals all around him, but he didn't fear they would upset the little boat. Rather, he was comforted by their presence, as if they promised safety. But safety from what? He was perfectly well-guarded, first among his new pack and then at SearchLight Academy, where nothing out of the ordinary ever happened.

Then someone approached Amaruq in another kayak. Even though he couldn't know, somehow he was sure this was another shifter, like him, and yet different. Amaruq transformed into a wolf when he chose. This shifter was... something else... when he changed.

The other's broad face and short stature called to mind all the pictures of Inuits he'd seen since he started trying to research his heritage, and of course the features reminded him of himself and his family. But where his family kept their hair neatly cut in Western style, this one's hair was wild as he pushed back the hood of his parka.

"Amaruq." He always knew Amaruq's chosen name without having to be told. "Come to the shore with me."

They reached land much more quickly than was possible but this never bothered Amaruq. They hauled their kayaks up on the beach so they wouldn't wash away. Then the shifter took off his gloves and cupped the sides of Amaruq's face. "You're handsome."

"What's your name?"

The shifter laughed. "You'll know when it's time." And he kissed Amaruq.

Over thirty and never been kissed before. I'm like that movie, Forty-Year-Old Virgin. Amaruq relished the kiss. It might only be a dream, but he felt sure real kissing would be just like this. Soft at first, gentle, persuasive, and utterly compelling. Then, as the shifter nudged Amaruq's lips open with his tongue, it was impossible not to fall into the play of mouths. As one tongue slid over another, touching teeth, and those same teeth nibbling the bottom of Amaruq's lip... His whole body woke with passion. He was wet between his legs. And, oh, even though he normally hated thinking of his sex, right now he adored the way the shifter made him feel. Like he was being lit up from the inside. Not as with fire, but as with a thousand fireflies. Or even the Northern Lights.

When his lover drew back, Amaruq was breathless with need. "Please," he whispered every time he had this dream. "Please..."

"What do you want? Tell me the truth."

"Your name."

The shifter tsked. "No, that's not what you truly crave. Tell me the truth."

And, as he always did, Amaruq confessed, "I want to know when I'll see you for real."

"Today."

This was such a divergent path from the usual ambiguous answer that Amaruq gaped. And he startled awake. It might have been the airplane's wheels hitting the tarmac that woke him, but he doubted it. His dream lover's startling promise was what did it. Looking down at his hands where they were fisted in his lap, Amaruq whispered, "Let it be today."

* * *

Nootaikok had been Tai to everyone since he joined SearchLight when he was eighteen. He was thirty-six now. His family called him by his full name; his tribe did the same. But to all his coworkers, from his most recent, short-lived partner to his supervisor, he'd been Tai. He honestly couldn't decide which he liked more, but he'd decided to embrace his full name this time around at SearchLight Academy. If he was going to make a new way for himself, he would do well to think of himself as a new person.

And the injuries he'd sustained in his former position as a tracker? He'd do well to think of those as birth defects. Something over which he had no control.

His empathy, the psychic gift he possessed, had saved his ass a number of times. But it hadn't been a failsafe.

Nootaikok pushed that thought away and returned to the one about birth defects. If he thought of his former life as influencing his current one as little as possible, he might overcome its demons.

Forcibly, he turned his mind back to the present. He had a roommate coming. SearchLight insisted everyone room with someone. Nootaikok knew a little about his coming headache. He also knew that was an unfair assumption, but he thought anyone who might get too close could be a problem. And roommates always saw more than he wanted them to. The kid's name was Amaruq Jones, a weird combination if ever there was one. He was a freshman and his former roommate, some human, had flunked out last semester.

Careful, he thought. *You're starting to sound prejudiced.*

Well, he sort of was. Humans needed protecting but they were their own worst enemy what with climate change, war, and the poverty cycle. A greater amount of Nootaikok's time had been taken up with protecting magical creatures from humans rather than the other way around.

And remember, you're not exactly an old pro at anything yourself, only being thirty-six. Compared to other trackers, who can live for centuries, you're a young'un even if you're almost middle-aged with a human-long lifespan. His tribe wasn't long-lived or anything. He was Inupiat, not a Night Wanderer or some similar Native-affiliated magical being.

Feeling like grumbling all day long rather than doing his unpacking, Nootaikok resolutely set himself to completing the latter. He wanted to be ready for classes on Monday and screw everything else. His past, the current situation, and the future too. Not to mention the nightmares. Those could permanently take a hike as far as he was concerned.

He'd do well to take this coming transition one task at a time.

It was a little unusual that Amaruq had been assigned a new room, but according to rumor, the human who'd been living with him had left quite a bit of negative psychic energy behind when he flunked out. This was Nootaikok's first semester, so he hadn't had a room to leave.

That, too, was unusual, starting halfway through the year. But Nootaikok wasn't a traditional student, having been to the academy once already.

When someone knocked on the closed dorm room door and then entered, Nootaikok didn't even look up from putting bedsheets on his longer-than-normal bed. *I swear, college beds all over the US are made with extra inches just to force us to buy specialty items.*

"Hi, Amaruq."

Silence greeted him and then the freshman answered, "Um, hi. How did you know it's me? Are you a precog too?"

Nootaikok looked up at the sound of that voice.

It didn't sound like a teenager's. His gaze locked with dark brown eyes in a narrow, small-boned face that was the color of coffee with maybe two tablespoons of cream. The features were older somehow, as if he'd seen quite a bit. His age certainly wasn't anywhere near eighteen. Nootaikok blurted, "How old are you?"

Amaruq blinked. "Um, thirty. Is that okay?"

Is that okay? What sort of question was that? *The question of one who is used to being judged and found wanting.* With this realization holding sway in his heart and calming the fire that had lived there since his tracker partner died, Nootaikok swallowed the half dozen terse responses he might have given and settled for something gentler. "I was given the name of my new roommate." He smiled and held out his hand. "I'm Nootaikok."

A huge smile lit up Amaruq's face as he took the proffered fingers in his own. "I'm pleased to finally meet you."

That word -- finally -- surprised Nootaikok. "Have you been waiting to meet me specifically?"

Amaruq nodded. He still held Nootaikok's hand and now he lifted it to his lips. He set three dry kisses along the knuckles. The softness of his mouth made Nootaikok shiver even as he hardened below the waist.

The slightly younger man said, "I've been dreaming about you for weeks. And I know you don't know me from Adam --" a brief look of frustration crossed his face --"but we're destined to be together."

Such a sweeping pronouncement went against everything Nootaikok knew to be true, but he was more interested in chasing the meaning behind that momentary expression. "What's wrong?"

Amaruq blinked at him, appearing genuinely confused.

"You had this weird look on your face when you said that I don't know you from Adam."

The same look came and went but then Amaruq laughed ruefully. "I hate using my parents' Western-gotten phrases, and 'don't know me from Adam' is one of them. There were no Adam and Eve in our heritage. At least not by those names. And even if my parents celebrate Christianity, that doesn't mean..." He stopped, looking embarrassed.

"You're Inupiat too?" Nootaikok guessed.

"Born one, but raised..." Amaruq shut his mouth.

Or, Nootaikok realized as he took in the other's form, her mouth. "Are you two spirit?" he asked.

Amaruq dropped Nootaikok's hand as if he'd touched something hot. "Didn't you hear me? I was born Inupiat but my family celebrates Western culture. Of course I'm not two spirit. I haven't approached any tribe. I don't want to until I know more about my heritage. And since no tribe has been allowed to accept me, let alone my gender identity, I can't be named two spirit."

Nootaikok nodded, accepting the rebuke. "I admit, I was assuming you'd at least been introduced to a tribe and made part of their community." He guessed, "Your parents don't approve of your gender identity?"

"Not at all." He was silent for a moment and then added, "I'm physically female."

"Is 'he' the right pronoun to use?"

It had been the correct question to ask. Nootaikok watched Amaruq relax. "Yes," the younger man answered and he smiled again, although not as radiantly as before. "I know there are transgender people who are nonbinary, but I'm not one of them."

Now that *that* was behind them… "You said you dreamed of me. Of your new roommate?" He didn't think that was what Amaruq had meant, but he didn't want to make any assumptions. Besides, maybe given this chance, Amaruq would rethink.

Amaruq shook his head. Then he laughed. "Maybe I should start unpacking. Monday's going to be here before we know it." He added shyly, "We can still talk while I'm working."

Nootaikok nodded and gave an encouraging smile.

"I didn't dream about you knowing you were my new roommate," Amaruq began as he moved his three suitcases from in front of the door. "I dreamed of my prophesied mate." He flashed Nootaikok a nervous grin before turning his attention to the first suitcase, which he lifted and set on his naked mattress. "I know how ridiculous that sounds, but if you'd seen the dreams I've been having…"

Mate. Nootaikok's erection began to reverse itself. Nootaikok knew all about dreams. He didn't give *his* dreams much traction, or tried not to. But a precog's dreams were different. "I'm not mate material," he said. "Not the way werewolves view mates." If he'd even been looking for a partner in love, his nightmares would have prevented him from getting close to anyone.

Amaruq's shoulders were tense when he answered, "Werewolves are different now. Our new alpha, Tilthos Charles, has said everyone has the freedom to have sex without instantly having to be bound together for life."

Maybe that was what the new alpha of the werewolves had said. Amaruq looked like he was telling the truth. But he also seemed to be uncomfortable with that fact. Probably because he'd been brought up with the normal werewolf tradition of sex equaling marriage. What the wolves called mating. "All right," Nootaikok allowed, "but you said 'prophesied mate', not 'prophesized lover'." Not wanting to seem like he was staring, he turned and began taking out the texts he'd bought at the academy's bookstore.

"I guess…" That apologetic, afraid of being hurt, tone had entered Amaruq's voice again. "I didn't mean mate."

Liar, he thought. But he didn't have the insistence on truth that werewolves did so Nootaikok kept his mouth shut.

"I just…well, I was hoping… if we hit it off…"

"I'm not mate material," Nootaikok said again, more gently. He could feel how disappointed Amaruq was by those words. His empathic ability gave him glimpses into the other's emotions. "But," he added after a moment of silence as he glanced discreetly over one shoulder and took in Amaruq's tight ass in his sprayed-on jeans, "I wouldn't be opposed to having sex. As long as you understand that if things go south between us, we still have to share a room. We have to be adult enough to do that."

Amaruq chewed his lip. "I need to be honest. I want you in my life. I've been dreaming of you for months. But I can be adult about this." He squared his shoulders resolutely. "I agree. How about no-strings-attached sex?"

I could get behind that. No pun intended. Although I'd have to be careful. Amaruq's heart is too obviously on his sleeve. "Sure. Let's finish getting ready for our semester and then screw like rabbits." He deliberately chose something crude, hoping it would help Amaruq see where he, at least, was coming from.

Amaruq was silent for several seconds. Then he asked, "You're not... uncomfortable... with the idea that I'm a man in a woman's body?"

"I'm attracted to both genders, but more to personality." *And yours makes me want to take care of you and make sure you lose that beaten-up attitude.* Nootaikok purposely kept this to himself. No one liked hearing that they looked like the culmination of a rough past. *Of any past really. Just look at me.* But he didn't want to look at himself. So, he said, "I can't wait to see if you shave your legs -- or anything else."

Chapter Two

Amaruq finished making his bed and glanced over at Nootaikok, who had been quietly reading for the last forty minutes. Not completely unpacked but increasingly aware of the wetness between his legs, Amaruq asked, "Are you ready?"

Apparently, Amaruq thought, *my disappointment that he doesn't want to mate right away isn't going to discourage my body.*

Nootaikok stood... and his arousal was very much in evidence. He looked slightly embarrassed when he glanced down at himself. "It's the sight of you lifting and moving things that's got me all hot and bothered."

"I could smell your arousal," Amaruq admitted. "That's... that's why I don't want to finish unpacking until later. Or tomorrow. Can you, ah, smell me?"

"I'm a narwhal shifter. Intense sense of smell isn't among our gifts." Nootaikok smirked, not unkindly. "But I can hear your heart hammering away in your chest. How long has it been since you've been laid?"

Amaruq felt himself blushing. "Never," he admitted. "But," he added quickly, not wanting to frighten Nootaikok away, "I broke my hymen while riding horseback years ago. And I've definitely... played with toys."

Nootaikok caressed himself through his pants and his erection stood out even more, tenting the khaki fabric. Then he smiled and there was gentleness as well as need in his expression. "I'll gladly be your first. You didn't happen to bring lube, did you?"

"To possibly meet my intended? Absolutely." Then his teasing tone vanished. "But I need to know, did you bring condoms? I do not intend to get pregnant and have to run back to my parents."

Nootaikok cursed. "I completely understand that, but I wasn't planning..." He started for the door. "Give me twenty minutes. I'll go to the nearest market..."

Amaruq found it charming that he'd said "market." "I'll be ready when you get back."

Nootaikok shot him a look. "What are you going to do?"

Amaruq tried to be flirtatious and wondered if he succeeded. "Play with myself."

Nootaikok's dark eyes, almost black, widened. Then he grinned. "Then I'll try to make it back in fifteen." He left with alacrity.

Amaruq began stripping at once. When he'd said he was going to play with himself, he wasn't kidding. He wanted to be all but dripping wet when his almost-lover came back. Amaruq admitted he'd been expecting to meet another precog, someone who would take one look at him, cry, "It's you!" and fall into his arms. He was hurt, and a little off-balance, but he wanted to enjoy whatever Nootaikok had to give. Even though their first meeting hadn't gone the way he'd expected, the fact that Nootaikok was willing to have a friends-with-benefits relationship boded well for a stronger friendship in the future.

Didn't it? He swallowed. *Didn't it?*

No thoughts like that. Time to show him how gorgeous you are.

He took off his boots first. They weren't the ones he'd worn most of his life, the ones designed to look feminine and keep his feet warm. These were meant for traipsing around on campus. Then, with them gone and tucked neatly under his bed, he removed his socks, tossing them in the hanging hamper he'd set up not half an hour ago. The socks were workman's socks, thick and meant to protect his feet from blisters. Next, he peeled off his jeans. They were skintight, one of the only articles of clothing he'd brought from his former life, because they looked good on him with any kind of top.

After stripping out of his underwear, he considered his muscular, well-made legs and smiled. Nootaikok had asked if he shaved. He didn't. Well, not his legs. But he did shave his pussy. Not because men shaved their nether regions but because he'd been preparing for Nootaikok since the dreams had started. It was rumored that men didn't like to "eat beaver" when that beaver was furry. And since Amaruq had always hoped to be eaten out, he wanted to make it as pleasurable as possible.

He wetted a finger and slipped it between the labia. He *was* quite dewy, as silky and dripping as a grassy morning in midsummer. He lifted his fingers to his nose, scenting himself. His aroma wasn't particularly strong and he liked that. Apparently growing up as the child of health nuts was good for something.

He dipped his fingers back down and caressed the nubbin of flesh that gave him such pleasure even as it labeled him as what he didn't want to be.

Amaruq firmly set his mind on his body's needs and off of what he was not. He would never be able to transition, so he'd better get used to it.

Never say never. He smiled a little as he continued to play with his clit. *Werewolves live a good long time, not affected by age but by their short tempers. There's nothing to prove that the technology and know-how won't come eventually.* Mood bolstered and the working of his fingers working miracles, he closed his eyes and pictured Nootaikok. The slightly older man's hair was black as Amaruq's own, but there they diverged. Amaruq was about three-quarters Inuk, the singular form of Inuit. He had lighter brown eyes than most of his family and definitely lighter irises than the culture to which he believed he should belong. His face wasn't as broad as Nootaikok's and Amaruq didn't like that about himself. And despite being born female, he was marginally taller than his with-benefits friend.

All right. And I need to stop thinking about what I lack or I won't be ready for Nootaikok when he comes back. Amaruq pressed his clit firmly, relishing the spark of pleasure that shot up from between his legs. Then he resumed undressing. He took off his long-sleeved T-shirt, which said "Hidalgo" on it, naming one of his favorite underdog movies. Then he pulled off the tight tube top he'd worn beneath his undershirt to keep his breasts flattened. He was grateful that he was only a B cup. He could be like the other transgender female to male wolf who lived in Tilthos Charles's house, Conrad. That particular wolf had size DD breasts and frequently complained about the difficulty of hiding them. *Although it must be admitted that Conrad's lover, Josephine, seems to like his breasts, bound or unbound.*

Tits now free, Amaruq stood completely naked. He ran a hand through his short hair, fluffing it. Then he went in search of his dildo and lube.

* * *

Nootaikok walked in on a one-person orgy.

Amaruq was a sculpted god, from his narrow-chinned face, down over his muscular chest and six pack, and right to the low-arched soles of his finely fashioned feet. He was paler where the sun and wind hadn't touched him on a regular basis and Nootaikok found this charming. But what he really enjoyed was the way Amaruq was reclining on his, Nootaikok's bed, and smoothly gliding a dildo in and out of his pussy.

The lighter brown of Amaruq's eyes seemed brighter, hotter, as he concentrated. His nipples were peaked and his lips were parted and wet.

Nootaikok locked the door before crossing the room and setting the plastic bag of condoms on the desk on his side of the room. He toed off his sneakers and watched with pleasure and satisfaction as Amaruq's gaze snapped to him. The wolf shifter stilled, the dildo half out of his pussy, and watched with obvious interest.

Stripping out of his thin sweater, Nootaikok dropped it over the back of a chair. Then he took a moment to play with his nipples through the barely-there fabric of his undershirt. He groaned softly when Amaruq pulled the dildo free and tossed it onto the other bed before standing and walking, naked, toward him.

They stood, facing each other, Amaruq about two inches taller, toe to toe. Amaruq put his hands, palms flat, on Nootaikok's chest. His lips were parted still and he darted his tongue out across the lower one.

Closing the distance, Nootaikok captured Amaruq's mouth with his own. He slid his hands around the slighter man's waist and then dropped the left to cup the narrow, masculine ass. Amaruq was built like a man in general. His body formed a T, with broad shoulders and a trim waist. No curve of hips or butt. Excluding his breasts and the inviting opening between his legs, he resembled a man more than a woman.

Abruptly, Nootaikok's thoughts were derailed as

Amaruq cupped his balls through his khaki trousers. He moaned and thrust into the air.

Amaruq closed his fingers lightly around Nootaikok's nut sac. "I want you. Strip faster."

Nootaikok obeyed, losing trousers, socks, and boxers in moments. He retreated enough so he could snag a condom out of the bag he'd brought in. He unwrapped it and expertly rolled it onto his engorged sex.

Amaruq glanced at the dildo with which he'd been pleasuring himself. "About the same size." He grinned. "Being a precog has its advantages."

"So does being an empath." There was no question that Amaruq was more excited than nervous. Aside from his peaked nipples and the barely detectable smell of his arousal, there were the waves of emotion flowing off him. Need. Lust. And a desire for simple touch.

Nootaikok dropped to his knees and began kissing his way up Amaruq's right thigh, starting at the knee and moving all the way up to the hip. When Amaruq shivered, he paused. "Okay?"

"Very much okay."

Nootaikok nodded. He'd felt as much through the empathic sense he had, but it always paid to get verbalizations. People didn't like to think you were reading them without their permission and making assumptions. Even if the guesses you made were based on fact.

He began kissing his way up Amaruq's left leg and had the pleasure of feeling Amaruq's desire for sensual caress spike. He cupped his bedmate's ass in both hands.

Amaruq jumped. But then he said, "That feels wonderful. I've never had someone touch me like that."

If that was true, they would have to go slowly. Nootaikok stood up, circled his bedmate, and began massaging Amaruq's shoulders. They weren't tense, but under his ministrations, Amaruq started to melt. It was a beautiful sensation, feeling the wolf respond. He sighed with obvious pleasure and murmured, "You don't have to, but I'm glad you are."

Nootaikok smiled. He moved his hands down Amaruq's back, kneading and caressing. "Tell me what you want."

"You inside me," Amaruq confessed, and the truth of that statement was strong in the air. He laughed nervously. "I know that makes me sound like a wanton whore, but --"

"Never. It makes you honest." Nootaikok slapped Amaruq's ass very lightly. "And that's for calling yourself a name that I'd never call you." He paused. "Unless we discover, over time, that you like dirty talk. But that wasn't meant as anything but a disparagement. You are allowed to express your lusts as well as your fears."

"You're wonderful."

"And I was a virgin at one time too. So, give yourself a break."

"All right."

Nootaikok knelt in front of Amaruq again. "If that's what you want, me inside you, we still have a little more prep to do. Spread your legs and bend your knees a little."

When Amaruq had complied, it was easy to slip between his parted thighs. Nootaikok tasted him and he tasted lightly of female but more of wolf. His scent was subtle and his fluid was heavenly.

Nootaikok licked the nubbin of Amaruq's sex.

Then, as the wolf shifter moaned above him, he let go of the narrow left asscheek so he could slip two fingers into the waiting vagina.

At once, Amaruq began to rock on his digits.

Nootaikok removed them soon after and then stood. "Top or bottom?"

"Aren't you going to... Well, aren't you going to be inside me?"

He smiled a little. "Yes, but that doesn't require the missionary position. If you'd like to straddle me..."

Amaruq appeared to give it serious thought. Then he said, "No, I want you on top of me."

So, they moved to the bed, where Amaruq settled on his back and spread his legs. Then, when Nootaikok climbed on top of him, he wound them around the available waist. "Fuck me."

Nootaikok took himself in hand and slipped between Amaruq's parted thighs. He looked deeply into Amaruq's eyes and saw passion and lust warring in their depths. *By all the gods, he already loves me.* It was a sobering thought, or it should have been. Instead, his balls tightened and he pushed into the waiting heat of his bedmate's receptive body.

When he was fully seated, he waited a few breaths for both of them to adjust. There wasn't a trace of pain on Amaruq's face and Nootaikok marveled that he was, in fact, a virgin. Then he began to thrust.

Soon, he discovered that angling slightly to his right caused the greatest pleasure for his partner. He was obviously stroking some secret place that made Amaruq's eyes cross and his breath come faster. Nootaikok listened to the rapid beat of both of their hearts as he moved, pressing deeply and firmly. He balanced on one hand and both knees so he could use the index finger of his right to caress Amaruq's clit.

His partner's first orgasm took him by surprise; he watched in fascination as Amaruq's lips were drawn back from his teeth, revealing his longer-than-standard canines. At the same time, the channel through which Nootaikok moved constricted, sending spikes of need through his whole body. He moved faster, letting off of Amaruq's clit.

His partner's second orgasm was also Nootaikok's and they rode out the mind-blowing pleasure together. Nootaikok cried his bedmate's name, but softly, aware that there were other students present who would surely hear if he was too loud.

His whole body shuddered with the power of his release.

He collapsed on top of Amaruq for a moment but then, aware that he might be heavy, pushed himself up. Or tried to. Amaruq tightened sinewy arms around his back and kept him down.

They lay together for several minutes. Then Amaruq murmured, "I want to do this every day."

"Me too," Nootaikok admitted. "I think we can manage at least once a day." He chuckled. "Or more, assuming our studies allow it." He glanced at the clock on his desk, saw it was an hour until dinner would be served in the hall halfway across campus, and asked, "Do you want to sleep a little?"

Amaruq smiled. "You read my mind."

After Nootaikok got up and stripped off the condom, they snuggled. Amaruq fell asleep first, based on his deep and even breathing. But Nootaikok soon followed.

And, for once, there were no nightmares.

Chapter Three

It was Saturday again, a week and a day since Nootaikok had slept with Amaruq for the first time. They hadn't quite made their commitment to have sex every day, but they'd managed five times. Searchlight Academy was as demanding as Nootaikok had remembered. It had been a whirlwind week, stealing moments to touch Amaruq when they were both studying. He loved the way Amaruq gave as good as he got, learning quickly the places that made Nootaikok shiver. Like, for example, how Nootaikok liked his cheeks kissed. It was probably a holdover from being in narwhal form, but his face was sensitive to kisses.

It was technically Sunday, he thought when he glanced at his clock. After that first glance, he lay completely still in his bed while the stench of sweat rose all around him and his heart thudded. His eyes were closed, not because he found comfort in the darkness but because he was trying desperately to calm himself down, and being aware of his body was one way to do that.

The nightmare hadn't been anything new, but that didn't lessen its power. It was the first time he'd suffered the images of death since he'd started sleeping near Amaruq. Even if they didn't share a bed, Amaruq's presence was comforting. Or maybe, Nootaikok's practical side argued, he was just too exhausted after sex to have bad dreams.

But in his experience, nightmares came whenever they wanted. It was most likely the reassurance of having Amaruq close that held them at bay.

In the dream, he'd been standing between huddled hostages and the crazy, possibly rabid, werewolf. Bernard was the wolf's name and Nootaikok had used it frequently, gently, to help form a connection with the mad magical creature. It seemed to be working too.

Until one of the hostages lunged for the wolf's gun. Not understanding that this wasn't a human, like her, the woman had taken a calculated risk. Because of how she had been acting, protective of the others and submissive, neither Nootaikok nor Bernard-the-possibly rabid-wolf had expected such a move from her. If her opponent had been human, the ploy and sudden attack would probably have worked. But Bernard was a wolf, quicker than humans and much stronger. He'd snapped the woman's neck and thrown her into Nootaikok's arms. Then he'd ordered Nootaikok, at gunpoint, to take her out of the room because, he claimed, he couldn't "abide" the scent of dead humans.

Nootaikok had sensed, empathically, the partial lie. Bernard was conscious that he was lying. But he was also aware of the wolf's desperate need, no matter its origin, to get the corpse away from him. He'd negotiated, asking to take half the hostages with him.

Bernard had agreed, promising to wait until Nootaikok came back and negotiated the release of the rest. Nootaikok had believed him. Empathic ability told him the wolf wasn't lying. And, all these months after, he knew Bernard hadn't lied. He'd changed his mind, but in that moment, he'd honestly believed he would wait.

Nootaikok had taken the hostages he could out of the building, silently apologizing to those he couldn't take this first trip. He and the humans were only about a dozen steps outside the building when the whole place blew up, throwing Nootaikok several feet and killing two out of the five hostages he'd managed to get out.

Now, laying in the dark with his eyes closed and his heart thundering beneath his ribs, Nootaikok asked himself again, *How could you have been fooled? How?*

And, the corollary to that: *How can you ever trust yourself to go into a similar situation?*

Simple, the answer. He couldn't.

The problem had been, his superiors assured him, that he hadn't talked to his tracker partner. He seemed convinced that his partner would have known. Safely six months from that terrible day, he wasn't so sure.

Jared had died while watching over the other half of the hostages. The only reason Nootaikok was back at SearchLight Academy was that he thought he could be helpful in some less-dire capacity. And working among humans... well, he didn't like hiding who he was, so working among those who didn't know about the existence of werewolves wasn't an option to his way of thinking.

"Nootaikok?"

He stiffened as Amaruq's voice came out of the darkness. He didn't answer, holding himself perfectly still. But his heart continued to gallop like a panicked stallion.

The bed on the other side of the room creaked.

Nootaikok thought as hard as he could, *Don't come over here.*

If Amaruq had any trace of telepathy, he'd be able to pick up on the thought. But either the wolf shifter didn't have telepathy or he was choosing to ignore it because he crossed the room, his feet making a quiet shuffling sound on the linoleum. Neither did he simply stand beside the bed or sit. Instead, he crawled under the covers, wrapped his arm tightly across Nootaikok's chest, and began to sing.

His voice was low in pitch and timbre but he didn't sing an Inuit song. He somehow knew a Werewelsh love song.

Listening in the depths of his discomfort and confusion, Nootaikok focused on the words as a way to cement his perception in the real world rather than the one of the dream. He translated with difficulty since the language was one he'd acquired rather than grown up with.

> *In the chill of Winter's howl,*
> *I cuddle close to you.*
> *I seek the warmth of your touch*
> *And harmonize with the wind.*
> *Oo, oo, oo, oo*
> *I need your arms around me.*
> *The wind sings such a sad song.*
> *Protect me from the chilly Winter cry*
> *And I'll protect you*
> *From what stalks your dreams.*

When the words were done, Amaruq continued to hum the melody as he rubbed circles over Nootaikok's chest and belly. The predictable movement was soothing and gradually Nootaikok's heartbeat slowed.

He opened his eyes and saw Amaruq's face. The wolf was exuding calm and peace and his expression reflected that. He seemed to find nothing unusual about calming a former SearchLight murderer-for-pay after a nightmare.

But he doesn't know about my former life. That's why he's so calm around me.

Nootaikok vowed to never tell Amaruq what he used to be. Maybe he couldn't avoid the memories, but he could certainly keep from inflicting the truth of his past on an innocent. And Amaruq was innocent, no matter his rough past. He had never killed. He had never lost people on his watch.

Amaruq started another song and he used his free hand to stroke the hair back from Nootaikok's forehead in an impossibly tender gesture.

Nootaikok's heart swelled with gratitude, but still, it was hard to receive such tenderness. He felt like he hadn't earned it. He considered pulling away, but really there was nowhere to go without kicking Amaruq off the bed and he couldn't quite bring himself to lose the contact with the gentle wolf. Not when his simple movements were so comforting.

The mountain you're climbing is just a pebble.
The ocean you're crossing is just a puddle.
The sky you're trying to reach is just a kite -- pull it down.
And the hand you're holding will never let you fall.

Again in Werewelsh, the tune was soothing and the way Amaruq sang it made the words seem less consonant-heavy as they normally were. Nootaikok closed his eyes and the images from his nightmare didn't leap forward to torment him. He sighed deeply.

"Do you have nightmares often?" Amaruq murmured.

"I... No." Then Nootaikok cursed. "I forgot. You're a werewolf. You can tell I just lied."

"It's obvious you did so to protect yourself." Amaruq kissed Nootaikok's ear. "It's all right." He moved his soft lips to Nootaikok's cheek and when he spoke his breath was warm and light. "You're not unique in having nightmares. They're completely normal. There's nothing wrong with you, that you dream about frightening things."

If you knew what I dream... But he felt the pressure of Amaruq's hand pushing down firmly on his chest and his thought trailed away. It was like having a weighted blanket, and although he had never slept with one of those, he'd sat with one pooled on his lap and remembered the sensation fondly.

"There's nothing wrong with you because you dream."

He *knew* that. Of course he did. After six months of counseling, he'd better know it. But hearing Amaruq voice the truth had more power than any number of sessions with the therapist whom he'd never completely trusted. Sighing again, he felt the bed take his whole weight and the pillow absorb the full pressure of his head as his neck muscles relaxed. "Thank you."

Amaruq kissed his cheek again. "I'm going to..." He started to rise.

Nootaikok caught his hand. "Please. Stay. Sleep with me."

Amaruq hesitated. "I... I snore," he finally admitted.

Like Nootaikok hadn't heard that during past nights? "As if that bothers me?"

"I might... drool."

Nootaikok chuckled. "Bodily functions are never a reason not to sleep with someone." And because he had a feeling Amaruq was resisting because he, Nootaikok, hadn't chosen to share a bed with him after that first time, he added, "Please stay with me. I could really use the comfort."

Amaruq at last snuggled against his side. "Okay. Do you want me to keep singing?"

"I really liked that second song," Nootaikok

confessed.

"Do you speak Werewelsh?"

"I took it in… well, here at the academy. A lifetime ago. But I retained enough to understand what you were singing. Where did you learn?"

"I took a correspondence course through SearchLight Academy."

"I didn't even know they offered such things." They surely hadn't when he'd last been here. Of course, that was seventeen years ago.

"They don't offer many courses. But I'd already been in love with the sound of these songs, so learning their meanings was a pleasure." He paused. "Most of the world's magical languages are taught via correspondence course. But Werewelsh was the only one I wanted to learn." He chuckled softly. "It helped me skip some classes when I finally got here last fall." He settled his head on Nootaikok's shoulder and began to repeat the second song.

The next thing Nootaikok knew, it was morning and Amaruq's leg was thrown over his thigh. He smiled at the wolf's light snores. Then he grinned outright at the morning wood he'd woken with. It was stronger than usual, more fully erect. *And that's certainly because Amaruq's sleeping with me.*

* * *

Amaruq dragged his ass out of Introduction to Inuit Magical Creatures the following Monday, the second Monday of the semester. He was holding his quiz from Friday in one hand, unable to put it down. He'd failed. *Failed.*

He was a complete dunce. These were supposed to be his people. Hell, the only question he'd gotten right was the short essay about the legend of the narwhal. *But I studied that one for weeks before I even came to the academy. Because I was convinced my new mate would be found among narwhals.*

The biggest reason he'd failed was because he'd struggled to remember which things were facts, like how the werewolves had come to Alaska. Others were legends.

Stopping at a convenient table, he took the backpack off, opened it, and removed the appropriate binder. He put the quiz in it. Then he simply stood there for several moments, staring down at the forty percent on the top.

"Amaruq? Hey, what's wrong?"

He jumped, dropping the binder. Everything was going to fall out of it and --

Nootaikok caught the falling plastic. "Okay, now I know something's wrong."

Amaruq shook his head. "It's... It's not a big deal. I failed a quiz."

Nootaikok put an arm around his shoulders even as he slipped the binder back into the pack. "Come back to the room and we can talk about it."

Amaruq didn't want to talk. He wanted to have sex and forget the quiz had happened.

"Don't bother looking at me like that," Nootaikok murmured in his ear. "If you failed a quiz, you need study. Not sex."

"Can't I have both?"

Nootaikok laughed, keeping it low. "Absolutely. If you prove to be teachable."

Amaruq's sex tingled. He pressed his thighs together to increase the sensation.

An hour later, he wasn't sure he was proving to be anything like a teachable student. He was frustrated and anxious and annoyed. "It's all fluid!" he complained from where he sat on his bed with his legs crossed and his notes open beside him. "Werewolves came to Alaska in the late 1800s. I get that. And the people of Alaska didn't have werewolves, as such, in their society before then. But all these other shifters..." He shook his head. "Hell, even my taken name means more than just 'wolf'. It means some sort of wolf shifter that isn't a werewolf because... Why?"

"Because Amaruq shifters don't change with the full moon, but with the new." Nootaikok spoke patiently and that made Amaruq feel guilty for his outburst.

The other shifter stood, abandoning his place on the desk chair and crossing to Amaruq. "You've already learned quite a bit more than you knew when we first came in here. I think you just needed it presented in a new way, as a similar and contrast comparison set, rather than a list of every single species." He took the notebook off the bed and set it, closed, on Amaruq's desk. Then he turned back and smiled. "I think you deserve a reward for all of your hard work."

Much faster than the first time, mirroring the speed with which they disrobed as a matter of course now, they were naked. Nootaikok didn't encourage Amaruq to settle on the bed as he often did. Usually they began that way, but today he wanted something else. He began pleasuring the breasts that caused Amaruq so much embarrassment and annoyance most of the time.

Starting with the left one, he kneaded the flesh firmly. Then he took the slightly aroused nipple between his lips.

Amaruq groaned as stars seemed to explode behind his closed eyelids.

"Shh," Nootaikok whispered on a laugh. "You're

going to announce your enjoyment to the whole floor."

"They're not all werewolves," Amaruq protested, although he did so sotto voce.

"True, but did you know there are two werewolves right next door?"

Amaruq hadn't. He flushed. "How do you know they're werewolves? I thought you didn't have a keen sense of smell."

"I don't. It's more about their posturing and way of speaking."

Amaruq blinked, confused. "Do I have…" He groaned again, covering his mouth, as Nootaikok licked his right nipple.

"Yes," Nootaikok murmured, "but that's all right. I have characteristics unique to my people." He licked Amaruq's nipple again before returning to the left and actually nibbling it lightly.

Amaruq closed his eyes, unsure when he'd opened them, and allowed his whole body to be filled with sensation. Whatever "tells" he was giving away as a werewolf, he didn't care just then.

His attention was caught and held by the downward drift of Nootaikok's hand, over his stomach and down to the shelf above his pubic area. He sucked in a breath and parted his thighs. Feeling slightly off balance because of the pleasure Nootaikok was still bringing to his nipples, he clutched the other shifter's shoulders. Now, since he couldn't hold on and muffle his cries, he pressed his lips together firmly and tried to swallow each pleasure-induced sound.

"And I'm not even touching your clit yet," Nootaikok murmured. He rubbed his cock against Amaruq's thigh.

His uncovered cock.

I want his seed inside me. Someday. But not now.

"Condom?"

"I won't go inside you without it. Open your eyes and look at me."

Amaruq obeyed. He watched Nootaikok take the left nipple he'd been licking between his lips again. He watched Nootaikok peel his lips back from his teeth and take the nipple that way. His left eyetooth was slightly longer than his right. He nibbled a little more firmly and pleasure shot both up Amaruq's spine to blossom in his head and down to his clit. He moaned, forgetting to keep it behind his teeth.

"Maybe I should spank you every time you forget to smother your gorgeous noise."

Amaruq turned and presented his ass. "Although the wolves will definitely hear that too."

"Good point." Nootaikok crossed the room, grabbed his phone, and turned on some music. Then he raised the volume. "There we go. Much better." He strode back to Amaruq and slapped his ass.

Amaruq groaned without bothering to stifle the sound, and received another slap, as he'd been hoping.

Nootaikok rubbed his uncovered cock against Amaruq's ass. "Now I need to put a condom on."

He prepared Amaruq with two fingers. The sensation of being filled was like poetry in a foreign language: something Amaruq couldn't quite understand, but which filled him with music nevertheless. They were standing, Nootaikok behind him, pleasuring him with a hand between his legs. Only when Amaruq was shuddering and moaning almost nonstop did Nootaikok remove his fingers and roll the condom into place.

Amaruq rode Nootaikok, loving the new angle and the way Nootaikok's cock throbbed deep in his pussy. It was paradise. He rode the other shifter while

Nootaikok stroked his clit.

He came three times, twice before Nootaikok and once just after. Collapsing on top of his lover -- for surely they were lovers now, after he had soothed Nootaikok's troubled mind and had his own worries calmed -- he snuggled in and whispered, "I'll be a much better student now that we've played. I promise."

Nootaikok chuckled. "I wasn't counting on that, but if that's what it takes to make you study, who am I to argue?" He kissed Amaruq's cheek. "And, yes, we're lovers now."

Amaruq blinked, startled. "I thought you were an empath, not a telepath."

"Some questions are so loud with feeling that they come through." He nudged Amaruq's hip lightly. "Get off for a little bit. I have to lose this sticky condom. Then..." He kissed Amaruq's lips softly. "I want you to sleep with me."

Often after lovemaking, he'd sent Amaruq back to his bed or sought his own. Whatever had happened to change that tonight, Amaruq didn't argue.

Chapter Four

Nootaikok was dreaming about his therapy sessions of all things. The brownie who'd been assigned to his case was the gentlest kickass he'd ever met. She encouraged him to confront his feelings head-on and to take no prisoners, and yet she did so in the kindest way imaginable. He was aware that he was dreaming and yet her personality held sway as Dr. Cora Davies held his gaze and murmured, "There's a terrible time coming for you, but out of it will come the greatest joy. Be strong and set aside your doubts about the past."

"But I can't do that," he protested. "If I don't learn what I did wrong, I'll never know how to prevent it from happening again." Then he added, "Unless you mean to just forget it because I'll never be in that position again. Since I'm working to be an interdepartmental facilitator."

"You will face that challenge again, and you must forget its predecessor or you will freeze at a crucial moment."

He opened his mouth to argue and was distracted by a low moaning. "What's that?"

She didn't answer but now she seemed insubstantial.

Nootaikok fought his way out of the dream and up from the depths of sleep.

The first thing he was aware of was the body snuggled against him. Because it wasn't snuggled at all but glued to him, as if its owner was stuck to him by an electrical current.

Amaruq. The werewolf had fallen asleep next to him, had been doing so since the second week of January, which meant it had been almost a month. But never had he clung to Nootaikok with such desperate strength. And the werewolf was moaning quietly in his sleep.

Softly, not wanting to frighten his lover but needing to wake him, Nootaikok brushed the hair off the wolf's forehead and stroked his cheek. "Come on now," he murmured. "Wake up. Everything's all right."

For a moment Amaruq's grip tightened. But then he shuddered strongly and opened his eyes. "What... Where?" He shook his head a little without it leaving the pillow. "Nootaikok? What..." He winced as if something hurt. "Did I wake you?"

"Yes, but it was a good thing."

"Did you dream about the guns too?"

Aware that Amaruq was a precog, Nootaikok asked, "Guns? Tell me about that."

Amaruq hesitated. "It was probably nothing."

"Do you dream about guns and violence on a regular basis?" He knew this wasn't the case; Amaruq's nightmares were mostly about being ignored by some future Inupiat tribe because he was too "Western".

"No, but..."

"Then it's probably something important." He rolled over onto his side so he could meet Amaruq's dark gaze. "Tell me."

Maybe it was the firmly commanding tone or maybe Amaruq was used to obeying, but he responded without any more hesitation. "I dreamed about James and Chen and Brett and most of the other people in this dorm being held at gunpoint. You and I were there too and..." His breath caught and he coughed lightly into his shaking hand. "None of us could access our psychic powers. I don't know why."

"Were we wearing collars?" Nootaikok asked, thinking of the rumored technology the grand Fae were supposed to use to keep their prisoners under control. The collars only kept other grand Fae confined, or that was the scuttlebutt. But, he thought, anything used to restrict a grand Fae could probably be used on other magical creatures. The grand Fae, few in number though they were, were vastly more powerful than the majority of other beings.

"I don't know," Amaruq whispered, sounding miserable and afraid.

Nootaikok hugged him close. "Thank you for telling me. I'm going to talk to security. Just in case."

"But it's only a dream."

"With strangely specific images. And given by a precog." He nudged Amaruq gently. "Get up, please. I'll be back in twenty minutes or less. Are you willing to talk to security if they need a direct account?"

Amaruq nodded, looking dubious. "I doubt they're going to take it seriously."

"Why?" Nootaikok asked as he began getting dressed.

"Because... Well, because nobody in my family ever did."

"Your family's made up of Class A jerks."

Amaruq snickered but then his agitation returned. "Are you sure this is worth bothering them about?"

"Absolutely." He'd never lost the knack of being quick; it was like riding a bicycle. He'd already gotten into his jeans and sweater. Now he tugged on a pair of sneakers without bothering with socks.

"It's freezing out there," Amaruq protested.

Nootaikok pointed at him. "Werewolf." Then at himself. "Narwhal. A little cold doesn't bother either of us." He kissed Amaruq's cheek. "I'll be back. Lock the door. Just in case."

He hurried down the stairs and entered the lobby. He took a quick, reflexive look around, saw no one, and started across. The stairwell door creaked open behind him. "Amaruq, I told you --" He started to turn.

Something hard connected with the back of his head. Once. Twice. Nootaikok fell to his knees and tried to roll away from the attack.

He was stopped by a swift kick to the ribs. He groaned and curled in on himself, attempting to shield his head. Before the hard object connected with his head for a third time, sending him into darkness, he thought, *Amaruq. Let him call the authorities when I don't come back.*

He was sent into unconsciousness.

* * *

Someone pounded on Amaruq's door. He'd gotten dressed, mostly because he expected security people would want to talk to him and he didn't want to meet them with his breasts unbound. He felt uncomfortable meeting strangers without being fully dressed.

He started for the knob, reaching for it, and then froze as his dream asserted itself. "Who's there?"

"Security," came the immediate response.

Amaruq relaxed and opened the door. "Did Nootaikok..." He trailed off when he saw the grand Fae standing there looking at him. He inhaled to speak again and smelled silver. Then, belatedly, he saw the gun in the grand Fae's hand. *Calm down. Not all grand Fae are dangerous. We have some on campus here.* True, but were any of them in security? And since when did security officers go around in all black without even an insignia on their shoulder?

He tried to shut the door and the "security" guard raised the gun.

"Come quietly."

Amaruq hesitated but not because he didn't believe the threat implied in those two words. "Where's Nootaikok?"

"If he lives on this floor, you'll see him upstairs. Put your hands behind your back."

Amaruq considered transforming into a werewolf and bolting. But the door at the end of the hall had a doorknob that he couldn't turn easily while in lupine form. He'd be trapped on this floor. He put his hands behind his back.

Another black-clad figure stepped forward and closed a circle of metal around Amaruq's neck. Instantly, Amaruq felt his precog senses, which were always "on" even if they didn't feed him information, snap off. He staggered and the one with the gun jabbed the weapon against his solar plexus. "Come out."

Feeling weak and separated from the world, Amaruq obeyed. He was led upstairs with a group of three others, the ones he'd named to Nootaikok: James, the water dragon who was a senior now, Chen, James's roommate, who was a land dragon, and Brett, a half human-half Fae, although Amaruq didn't know what kind. All three of them wore collars that looked like they were made of metal and leather. Amaruq reached up and fingered his, finding it not made of silver. So, how could it suppress his abilities?

"Keep moving." Someone poked him in the back with the barrel of a gun.

He went up the stairs, the others ahead of him, all the way up to the top floor. The fifth floor didn't have any windows on one end. This was where they were herded. Before they entered the large room at the end of the hall, the one meant for dorm meetings, Amaruq smelled blood. His stomach churned.

They were urged through the doorway and into the room with its bare walls and nothing to grab or throw. Usually there were chairs in there, but these had been removed. *They thought of everything.*

Amaruq scanned the room, looking for Nootaikok. And when he spotted the narwhal shifter, his stomach did more than churn. It clenched and he uttered a soft cry.

"Quiet. Go sit down."

Amaruq ran to Nootaikok, dropping to his knees beside the shifter. Blood trickled from the back of Nootaikok's head and his hair was clumped with more of the same.

"What did you do to him?" Amaruq asked no one in particular. He glanced over his shoulder -- and recoiled when he saw a gun right in his face.

"Keep quiet. We don't need all of you."

Amaruq shut up. Then he settled on the floor, took Nootaikok's head carefully into his lap, and began stroking his lover's hair off the clammy forehead. *Nootaikok didn't make it to the security office.* He shivered. *I had my vision too late.* Guilt assailed him and he closed his eyes against the intensity of it.

"Is he all right?" Brett O'Connor settled beside him on the floor. His words were barely audible.

Amaruq opened his eyes and met Brett's concerned gaze. "I don't know." He dropped his voice even more and added, "Did you know they're grand Fae?"

Brett nodded. "I smelled blood-sucking vampires too. And as far as I can tell, there are about a dozen of them."

Amaruq counted the hostages. *That's what we are now*. He shivered. Most of his friends were here: Brett, Veronica, Andy, and the other five or six people who made up his close group of friends. Most were from his hall. But they weren't the only ones here. He counted at least three dozen students. *If it was just a matter of numbers, we could overpower our attackers. But they have guns. And they still have their powers*. He fingered the collar again.

"I wonder what they want," Brett mumbled.

In Amaruq's lap, Nootaikok groaned. But he didn't open his eyes.

How hard did they hit you? He glanced at Brett and tried to put on a brave expression. "I'm sure security will help us. We're in the middle of SearchLight Academy, surrounded by help."

Brett shook his head a little. "They got in. They're good, talented sons of bitches."

Amaruq sighed. Brett had a point. Feeling helpless, and wishing he'd had his dream last night, he went back to stroking Nootaikok's hair and waiting for his lover to wake up.

Chapter Five

When Nootaikok regained consciousness, he was aware at once of stomach-clenching nausea. This was to be expected, he reminded himself as he concentrated on keeping his breathing even in an attempt to combat the need to puke. *I was hit several times over the head. I'm just lucky I don't have a monstrous headache to accompany the upset stomach.* He opened his eyes, measuring his ability to sit up, and found that he was still too close to the edge to try.

His head was cradled in someone's lap. Without moving, he couldn't quite tell who it was. But he made a guess and his guts clenched. He prayed he was wrong, that they hadn't caught Amaruq too.

"Amaruq?" he asked quietly even as he spotted the shoes pacing back and forth several meters away. *Guards.* He didn't know that for sure, but the fact that he and whoever was holding him were on the floor and the other person was pacing argued for that conclusion.

"Thank the gods," Amaruq whispered. "How do you feel? Your bleeding has slowed."

Nootaikok touched the side of his head gingerly. Encountering no blood, he traced his skull to the back. Here he paused as his fingers encountered something tacky, and the pain he'd been successfully ignoring flared. "Well, at least they left me alive." He gathered his strength, preparing his stomach for the switch to vertical, and sat up.

The whole world swam and he closed his eyes, centering himself by the feeling of his palms pressed against the floor. His training was yelling at him to do something, to get innocents out of harm's way, especially to get Amaruq away from danger, but he couldn't do that until he could actually move without passing out or falling to his knees to puke. All trackers were living weapons. More than the guns or knives or anything else they carried, trackers *were* weapons. The fact that Nootaikok was retired didn't matter. But it did matter that he couldn't trust his body to support him. He'd have to wait until he was strong enough.

What he needed was sustenance. Lacking that, he needed to rally his resources, use the time he was immobilized to gather information, then strike at the best possible time.

"Maybe you should lay back down." Amaruq's voice was shivery.

Nootaikok took a good look at his lover and saw the wolf was badly frightened. *Well, and that's to be expected. We've been captured for some unknown reason and Amaruq's a civilian.* But when he glanced around, he saw he wasn't the only one watching Amaruq. His lover was being observed by most of the rest of the people from their floor. As if his anxiety was their own.

They look at him like a leader. Nootaikok had noticed Amaruq was extremely popular despite his hidden fears. He seemed to flourish among his classmates. Maybe because he was older, maybe because he was charismatic. But whatever the reason, his anxiety was theirs.

I have to find a way to keep them calm. He fumbled around for a topic of conversation that wouldn't alarm their guards. Taking Amaruq's hand, he asked, "Can you tell me something?"

Amaruq blinked, probably at the light tone of Nootaikok's question. "Sure?"

"Talk to me. Tell me about your family." He squeezed Amaruq's hand and looked deeply into his eyes, praying the wolf would go along with him. Talk without too much more hinting. *Let me do my job. Your job is to keep everyone calm.* He glanced around, catching the eyes of several fearful-looking students. "Come closer. I don't want Amaruq to have to speak loudly. We don't want to disturb our captors."

One of the assailants approached, waving his gun around. "What are you up to?"

"Trying to keep everyone calm," Nootaikok answered.

"What are you, some kind of tracker in training?"

That hit much too close to home. "I'm a therapist in training," Nootaikok answered easily. "If I keep everyone calm, you have less reason to shoot."

The creature nodded. "Good idea." And he walked away.

Nootaikok watched him go, trying to figure out by how he moved what sort of magical creature he was. If not for the collar around his neck, he would have known by empathic touch. Now, cut off, he couldn't be sure. And while it made sense that the being was a grand Fae since they were the ones with such technology, assumptions were not the right way to go.

Besides, he walks more like a blood-sucking vamp. All glide and less stalk.

He turned his attention back to Amaruq. "Please. Tell me the story." *So I can half listen and use the rest of my attention to figure out how we're going to get out of here.*

Amaruq nodded, glanced around, and said, "Sure." He even smiled a little.

"My parents are mostly Inupiat, but they chose to live in Anchorage instead of following the traditions set down by their ancestors."

A note of disapproval had entered his tone. Nootaikok, who had been discreetly looking at the guards and trying to decide if his suspicions were correct, glanced at Amaruq, because the wolf shifter sounded distressed. *Maybe this wasn't the best story to tell.* He opened his mouth to suggest a change in topic.

"It's all right, though," Amaruq went on. "I live with Tilthos Charles now."

"The alpha above all alphas," Sophia whispered. She was a werewolf from, Nootaikok thought, somewhere close to the Mason-Dixon line. "I hear he's really scary."

Amaruq grinned. "Not at all. I mean, he *is* intimidating at first. How can he not be, holding all that power? But he's got a great psychic vampire for a mate and..."

As he went on about the most powerful alpha in North America, James scooted close to Nootaikok. "You look like you're really paying attention to our captors. You need to know that one of them is a student. He's a grand Fae who threatened my lover back in December of last year."

"And he was allowed to remain?"

James smiled just a little. "He was provoked. My Hank has a temper."

Just then, one of the assailants stared at them. Nootaikok gestured James away and turned his attention back to Amaruq. He was pleased to see that many of the other students were clustering nearer and looked calmer. Amaruq was apparently a good storyteller.

"When I turned six, I had an argument with my parents about fish camp. Many of the students at school were raised in traditional tribes and all they talked about was fish camp." He smiled reminiscently. "I didn't get to go that year, but I snuck out the year I turned eight and got to spend four glorious days on the ice."

"Is everyone in your culture allowed to attend fish camp?"

"Absolutely. For my people, it's less about gender and more about what you enjoy doing. In a very real sense, there are four genders. Masculine men, feminine men, masculine women, and feminine women." He paused. "I think you should come up with questions to ask me while I talk to Nootaikok. And remember: nothing's off limits." He grinned engagingly.

Nootaikok moved carefully toward Amaruq, scooting on the floor so as to present a less threatening aspect. He'd noticed that the guards weren't paying a terrible lot of attention to their captives, but seemed to be talking among themselves.

Amaruq took Nootaikok's hand, leaned close, and whispered in a loving tone, "There are five grand Fae and seven vampires of the blood-sucking sort. One of the Fae is someone I've seen around campus. I don't know his name."

"James mentioned him," Nootaikok murmured back. "Can you point out which are vamps?"

Amaruq began to describe them by clothing, leaning his head against Nootaikok's shoulder and giving every appearance of flirting.

Nootaikok listened closely, grateful for Amaruq's ability to stay calm. It was almost like having another agent with him.

Then he chided himself for such a thought. Amaruq was a student, not an agent, and definitely not a tracker. He might be useful, but he was also one more hostage Nootaikok had to protect.

And yet he's more than that. He is important to me. Not as much as, say, he would if they were mated or bound, which was how his people talked of joining for life, but, yes, Amaruq was important.

And no matter how helpful he is, I must not think of him as a fighting partner.

Out of the corner of his eye, Nootaikok caught sudden movement among the hostiles. He turned his head and was confronted by three of the dozen approaching with guns. *Now what?*

"All the females. Get up."

Nootaikok started to rise, meaning to distract them somehow. He knew the glint in their eyes and his gut clenched at what that gleam meant.

The nearest assailant waved his gun at Nootaikok. "Sit down. Just the females."

Trembling, holding onto each other, the female wolves and lesser Fae and humans stepped toward the far wall.

"Anything you do to them will look bad for your cause," Nootaikok said.

"It's not a cause," the youngest of the group told him, his age obvious in the cracking of his voice. "It's a statement."

"And what is that statement?" Nootaikok pressed, hoping to play for time. The three hostiles had been joined by four more, leaving five to guard the door. Still too many to take on.

"That we can --"

"Shut up," snapped one of the others. He pointed his gun directly at Amaruq. "I'll shoot your boyfriend if you don't keep quiet." He glared at Nootaikok.

"Come on, bitch. Take 'em off."

Nootaikok closed his eyes and measured, mentally, the distance between himself and the assailant with the gun. Most bullets couldn't do a hell of a lot of damage. Yeah, they'd take him down.

Temporarily. Maybe for as much as an hour. But assuming the bullet either didn't hit him right between the eyes or directly through the heart, he would recover.

He couldn't let these innocents get raped.

The other hostiles had crowded around the males who were left behind, waving weapons in their faces.

Amaruq whispered, "At least some of them are loaded with silver."

Which made it more dangerous for the wolves among them.

Nootaikok opened his eyes and scanned the weapons. He noticed at least three were psychic resonators, which amplified a person's inherent psychic abilities so that they could render another person unconscious. Or kill them. He had no personal contact with blood-sucking vampires from his tracker days. He thought they had no psychic abilities, but he wasn't sure about that. The grand Fae had at least some mental power.

Two of the females, and he felt guilty that he didn't even know their species let alone their names, screamed.

Her pain was muffled a moment later. Nootaikok wanted to glare at the one holding a gun on Amaruq but it wasn't this one's fault that the females were being hurt. And glaring would only incur wrath.

Nootaikok's gorge rose. He had to do something.

He rolled to his left, in front of Amaruq, and bounded to his feet. His guts roiled and his head spun so badly from the blows he'd endured that he almost missed his mark. But his body took over even as it foiled his best swing. He connected a fist with the closest assailant's solar plexus. Then he wrestled the gun out of the other creature's weakened grip.

Before he had a chance to use it, three reports split the air. His head at once felt like it was in a vise and he dropped to his knees, unable to stay upright. He registered that he'd been shot by at least one bullet, but the real pain was in his head as the psychic resonator tried to scramble his brains.

Lacking access to his empathic talents, he still had the ability to mount his mental shields and he did so, cursing himself for not thinking of that ahead of time. If he'd been thinking straight… But now wasn't the time for self-recriminations. The only way he could save himself from a lethal dose of invisible energy was to go limp. He collapsed, not easing himself down, and felt his nose crunch against the rough, thin carpet. Not broken, at least he didn't think so because he could still breathe through it. Even if it was, let it be for now. He needed to act unconscious.

"Nootaikok!" Amaruq cried.

Please. Don't try to get to me. He waited, fearing more reports.

"Let me tend his injuries. Please."

"With what?" One of the assailants laughed.

"I'll bind his arm with my shirt."

"Fine. There always has to be one hero."

Nootaikok lay perfectly still as Amaruq began wrapping his arm. It hurt like a bastard, but unconscious people didn't scream or even wince. He channeled all his thoughts into staying still so he'd have another chance at the bastards.

"Hey! You're a girl!"

Amaruq cried out.

Nootaikok opened his eyes, needing to see, and realized they were dragging Amaruq away to join the other females they'd separated. *He had to stop them.*

"Stay down," whispered a voice he didn't automatically recognize. "There's nothing you can do. They'll kill you if you try."

Brett, a magical creature from Amaruq's circle. He lived on their floor and Nootaikok had never bothered to figure out what he was. Amaruq had said once he was Fae, but not what kind. Maybe he didn't know. Amaruq tended to judge people less on what they were and more on how they acted.

He assumed their assailants had heard the whispers and waited to be killed. But when no one approached, when some of hostiles started cheering, he realized Brett hadn't been heard.

Then a new scream rent the air.

Amaruq. He tried to push himself up.

Brett flattened a hand on his back and shoved him back down.

"We need a plan." That was James, the water dragon who dormed a few rooms down from Amaruq's and Nootaikok's.

"Yes," said a faintly accented voice Nootaikok finally identified as Chen, the land dragon who shared a room with James.

Chen went on, bending over and resting fingers against Nootaikok's neck as if taking his pulse. "We'll make them pay. But we need you thinking, not reacting."

Nootaikok ground his teeth but remained silent. They were right. He'd already taken multiple hits. If he kept causing trouble without a better M.O., he'd only get himself killed. That wouldn't help Amaruq.

But, by all the gods, it was terrible listening to his lover scream.

Chapter Six

Amaruq fell to his hands and knees, his nether regions on fire with agony and his breasts aching from mistreatment. He crawled to where Nootaikok lay with his eyes closed and his head pillowed in Brett's lap. "Is he..." Amaruq couldn't bring himself to say the word "alive."

"He's fine." Brett squeezed Nootaikok's shoulder.

But the other shifter had already opened his eyes. He gestured Amaruq closer.

Amaruq moved as near as he could and lay down, cushioning his head with his arm. A wave of dizziness and a need for oblivion swept through him. He fought it. He needed to know how badly Nootaikok was hurt. Because if his lover was in pain, Amaruq had a reason to put aside his own mounting terror, shame, and the myriad of other negative emotions threatening to drag him down.

He *would* collapse, and sometime soon. But he refused to do so where those who had attacked him could see.

To that end, he took Nootaikok's hand and squeezed when the other shifter, who surely couldn't be his lover now that he'd been raped, was looking at him.

"Don't even think that," Nootaikok whispered.

Amaruq blinked, startled and a little frightened. "You're wearing that damn collar. How can you know what I'm thinking?"

"It's something negative, it's probably something condemning yourself because that's what happens to victims of violence, and it's all over your face." He lifted Amaruq's hand to his lips and laid a gentle kiss on his knuckles. "You're still beautiful, you're still worthy of love, and don't you dare give in to what they want you to believe. You're stronger than that. Do you hear me? You're worthy of love no matter what they did."

Amaruq started to cry.

Nootaikok pulled him close, hugging him and rubbing his back.

Later, Amaruq wasn't sure how much time had passed but he had a feeling it had been a great deal, he drew back from Nootaikok and wiped his face, mopping off the tears and snot. He felt steadier although he hated that he'd cried in front of those who had humiliated him.

"You're handsome. Beautiful. Worthy of love."

Unsure what to say but determined to pull himself together, Amaruq sat up. He winced. "Bastards," he muttered. Then he laid back down with his lips against Nootaikok's ear and whispered, "The ones who are vampires will get sluggish as the sun rises. We should attack then."

Nootaikok stiffened. But then he turned his head and murmured back, "I won't risk innocents again."

"Again?" Amaruq raised his eyebrows and asked sarcastically, "And what are you? Police?"

He expected Nootaikok to snap back. Instead, the narwhal shifter answered, "Former tracker."

Oh shit. Granted, he only knew rumors of trackers, and the trackers he knew from Tilthos Charles's pack were kind. But… well, all trackers were licensed killers.

Amaruq swallowed his desire to pull away. What, exactly, was a former tracker doing at SearchLight Academy? Then he realized and his knowledge spilled out of him. "That's why you're having so many nightmares. Something happened to you while you were working."

Nootaikok answered, "Shh." He stroked Amaruq's hair.

"What can we do?" he whispered against Nootaikok's shoulder.

"Wait and see what their demands are."

Wait to be raped again? Damned if I will. Amaruq knew there were only seven vamps and five grand Fae guarding fifty hostages. But, like him, none of the hostages had weapons or even their psychic powers. He wondered suddenly what the assailants had done with the other five hundred plus students who lived in this dorm. It felt like his skin shrank as he realized the rest of the students might have been murdered in their beds. These weren't all the students from their particular floor, but about half of them. Maybe their attackers had only taken as many as they thought they could handle.

"What is it?" Nootaikok asked quietly.

Amaruq shared his concern.

Nootaikok hugged him. "I know." He rubbed Amaruq's back. "Let me handle this, okay?"

But you're not going to do anything but wait. Still, his mind whispered, maybe that was the best course of action.

Frustrated and antsy, Amaruq pushed his way to a sitting position. "I'm going to talk to the others. Make sure they're all right." He rested his head briefly on Nootaikok's shoulder when the other shifter sat up with a wince. "And don't give up. We'll find a way out of this."

"Let me handle it."

"If I find a way to escape, I'm taking it." Then he realized how that sounded. "If I can take anyone with me…"

Nootaikok touched his cheek, turning his head so their eyes met. "I'm not giving up. But these are armed and dangerous people. Don't get yourself killed."

* * *

According to the clock high on the wall of their prison, it was about an hour after sunrise. Nootaikok lay where he'd been for the last couple of hours, trying to regain his strength.

Or maybe that wasn't why he was lying so still.

He turned his thoughts from his physical state to the activity going on around him. Amaruq had been busy. He'd organized the captives into several smaller groups, each comprised of both males and females. The male magical creatures and humans were encouraged not to offer suggestions as was the typical thing for most of them, but to give comfort, which could mean anything from a hand to hold to gentle words. Amaruq, after this organization, sat with Brett and talked quietly. The intensity of Amaruq's gaze drew Nootaikok.

He's stronger than I thought. He's pushed the assault to the back of his mind and he's trying to do what he can for the others.

He would *not* make a good tracker. Only because his intentions shone too clearly on his face. Like right now. He was putting on a brave face for Brett and obviously channeling all of his energy into that. Yes, it was a mask, and that seemed to contradict Nootaikok's assessment, but a mask one had to work at versus a mask one didn't were two different things. Nootaikok was sure that the moment the circumstances changed, Amaruq's mask would drop away.

And yet, he felt love bubbling up inside him for Amaruq's show of bravery. He was obviously aware that the others were leaning on him and he was doing his best with the tools he had.

Unlike me.

But that was unfair. What tools did Nootaikok have? He had experience, true, but that only showed him that without a weapon, he was powerless.

I've worked without weapons, per se, before. Yes, but… Well, but nothing. He wasn't quite ready to fight hand to hand when fifty people might die, and there was an end to it.

He had his faking unconsciousness but that did nothing but keep the hostiles from shooting him again. They were wary of him so he'd blown the element of surprise.

What else did he have left? Nothing.

Well, all right, he remonstrated himself, I have my knowledge of the enemy. The vamps are definitely slowing down but that hardly helps. There were more vamps than grand Fae, but there were still five of the latter. And they were all armed.

He sensed someone close to him and opened his eyes, expecting to be confronted with the barrel of a weapon. Instead, Amaruq was settling down beside him and taking his hand. "How do you feel?" he asked in a normal tone of voice. Then, much quieter, "Brett and I have a plan."

"Better," Nootaikok replied in a moderate tone. But he glared at Amaruq and squeezed his hand, probably painfully.

Amaruq nodded. "Brett, Nootaikok wants to know about your mother."

Apparently this was the signal they'd agreed upon because Brett got up, crossed to them, and knelt beside Nootaikok. He whispered, "I'm a visionist." Then he launched into a story about a German-born frau who made the best this and that.

A visionist. Well, if he didn't have a collar on, that could be useful. Visionists were able to act like movie projectors, showing the world whatever was in their head.

He could fill this room with trackers. Wait. No. It would be obvious they were visions because how would the trackers have gotten in?

Nootaikok struggled to think of a way to interject his question. He cursed his slow wits, which were weighed down with the past. "What sort of, um, meat does your mother use?"

"Leprechauns," Brett replied promptly. He was grinning.

Nootaikok glanced at Amaruq, saw he was smiling too, and thought, *Leprechauns would work. Most of them can transport themselves anywhere in the world, depending on their strength. And since about two-thirds of them are lesser Fae, and many do work for SearchLight...*

He smiled. But now. How to ask...

Stop this. You don't know enough.

I do, he argued with himself.

If you're wrong, these fifty people will die. And Amaruq will be among them.

His gut clenched. He tightened his hold on Amaruq's hand. *I can't lose him.*

Amaruq nodded though as if he knew what Nootaikok was thinking. "Imagine it," he whispered. "Leprechauns invading."

Nootaikok closed his eyes, shutting out the world. He didn't want to risk it. But if he didn't what horrors would be visited upon these innocents? "I could offer to take him out as a sign of good faith for the negotiators."

"Not you," Brett whispered. "You're already

under suspicion." Then he chuckled and threw his arm around Amaruq. "I have a better idea," he said heartily.

Several of the females started crying loudly. The males increased their comforting, speaking over the sound of the weeping and wailing. It was quite noisy.

Again, they managed to convey a signal. Nootaikok felt his tension growing but he saw the advantages of their plan. "Okay," he said. "Amaruq takes you up there."

"I even offer myself to the guards," Amaruq murmured.

Nootaikok whispered fiercely, "No."

"Nothing will come of it. The instant they take off his collar..."

"What other fighters do we have?" Nootaikok asked. "Just to make sure they're ready to leap into action if your request is denied."

Amaruq and Brett glanced at each other and grinned with obvious relief. Then Amaruq began listing those who were studying to be trackers or those with special training under their belt or even those who'd fought outside of school. There were almost twenty.

"And you," Amaruq finished. "If you're strong enough."

"I am." He sat up but slowly, feigning weakness he no longer felt as adrenaline rushed through him. "Gather them together. Keep the nonfighters to the back of the room." He squeezed Amaruq's hand again. "Be careful."

Chapter Seven

Amaruq stood and Brett moved with him away from the group. Before they'd gotten ten steps, one of the grand Fae approached them. The vamps were all leaning against the wall, conscious but not really paying attention to what was around them. This was definitely their best chance for escape.

Instead of smiling disarmingly, Amaruq allowed his fear to show and retreated a pace as the gunman waved his weapon in Amaruq's face. To Amaruq's right, Brett also backed up a little.

"What do you want?"

Amaruq wondered why all the grand Fae and vamps were male. He hadn't noticed that until now. *Maybe they were always planning to rape us and didn't want their females to see.* He didn't have to feign a shiver. "I'm training to be a negotiator," he said quietly. "We were thinking that I could act as a shield and Brett as the hostage you could let go. As a sign of good faith."

"And why would we want to show good faith?"

"Because we wouldn't tell that you raped some of us."

"That doesn't matter," the grand Fae answered.

"It might," said one of the others who had drifted over to listen. "We might get our demands met more quickly if we were seen as more humane."

The first grand Fae scowled. "You've been tossing 'humane' around like a damn flag. If they think we're dangerous --"

"There's a difference between 'dangerous' and 'a force to be reckoned with'," Amaruq said softly.

The second grand Fae nodded. "Listen to him. He's being wise."

Now all the grand Fae were around them and most of them had lowered their guns and other weapons. "Do you speak for all those bitches we raped?" asked one of the gathered guards.

Amaruq hid a wince. "I do."

"It wouldn't cost us more than one hostage," said the one who'd been trying to persuade the others since the beginning. "The benefits far outweigh the possible deficits."

"We can't let them see the collars," said another grand Fae. "If they get their hands on that technology, they might figure out how to counter it."

"So, we take their collars off." This was from the first grand Fae. He looked as though he were thinking it over. "Sure, why not? It's not like we'd be releasing one of the real bitches."

"Maybe if we stopped calling them that…"

"Oh, shut up, you're already getting what you want." The first assailant reached out and snapped off Amaruq's collar. Then he reached over and did the same to Brett's.

Nootaikok was going to attack. Amaruq felt it like a figurative ice pick between the eyes. He threw himself on the closest grand Fae.

Then all hell broke loose.

* * *

The visionist was ready. The moment Nootaikok saw the collar come off, the room was lined with Leprechauns against three walls. All of them were armed and all of them spoke as one. "Drop your weapons."

Nootaikok moved before the grand Fae or sleepy vamps could put together the improbability of all those people speaking at the exact same moment without even a little overlap. He tackled the nearest hostile, which proved to be a tired-looking vamp. He stole the gun, glad it was a gun and not a psychic resonator. Then he grabbed the vamp by the chin and the top of the head, jerked his hand upward, and broke the magical creature's neck. But with his head still attached, he'd recover. Nootaikok didn't want to take the chance that an assailant would come back to haunt him. He dropped the vamp, stepped on his chest, and ripped his head off. It hurt, narwhal strength or not, and Nootaikok knew he'd be feeling it tomorrow.

Amaruq had taken out the nearest assailant, but he was sorely pressed by a vamp and a grand Fae. Brett, who had lost the Leprechaun vision, was trying to fight off two of their captors but he was losing the battle.

That was when the rest of the students, even those without training, surged forward. Nootaikok lost sight of Amaruq and prayed he was okay.

If I lose him, no matter what else happens here today… That would be too high a price.

He moved on to the next hostile, taking him from behind, not with the gun, which he'd stowed in his waistband after engaging the safety, but with his bare hands because they were more efficient. He snapped this one's neck too.

Then he heard Amaruq scream and all his tracker training took a backseat to his need to be at his lover's side. He shoved people, assailants and students alike, out of his way until he saw Amaruq. His lover was bleeding from a wound to the side of his head and he was on his hands and knees with one of the grand Fae standing over him with a psychic resonator.

Everything went into slow motion. Nootaikok shouted, "Drop it, motherfucker," not in the hopes of the grand Fae doing so, but because he might hesitate just long enough for Nootaikok to clean his clock.

It worked.

The grand Fae glanced at him for barely an instant. But that was long enough for Amaruq to grab the magical creature between the legs and squeeze. Then Nootaikok plowed into him, knocking him away from Amaruq and to the floor. The psychic resonator went flying.

Nootaikok didn't bother breaking the bastard's chin. Instead, he put his hands on either side of the grand Fae's neck and wrenched his head from his shoulders, using the narwhal strength within him. He took the time to chuck the head at one of the vamps, causing that worthy to be distracted long enough for James and Chen to take him down together.

He wanted nothing more than to check on Amaruq, but if he didn't make sure all the assailants were down he'd just be opening up the way for trouble. He stood, scanned the room, and saw that everyone who should be on the floor was. There were also some obvious injuries.

James and Chen approached him like lieutenants coming to their captain. "Collect all the weapons. Then move all the hostiles against that wall." He pointed. "Find out if we have any medics in training and see if they can help the wounded."

They nodded and set about their tasks. Nootaikok went to the door and shouted through it, "Tracker coming out. Tracker." And he opened the door.

To find half a dozen weapons leveled at his chest, but with the fingers of their bearers outside the trigger rings.

It was over. Now he could go back to Amaruq.

He rushed back into the room and completely

ignored all the controlled havoc around him as he dropped to his knees and took Amaruq's shoulders gently in his hands. "Amaruq? Can you hear me?"

Stunned eyes met his. "Yes..." He was shivering now.

He's falling into shock. "Keep talking. Tell me anything."

Amaruq smiled a little even as he continued to tremble. "You're hot when you're ripping heads off." Then he pitched forward and threw up all over Nootaikok.

That was okay. It was just so good that Amaruq was alive to be able to puke.

* * *

Amaruq sat with the entire student body in the dining hall, which was the largest meeting place on campus. He held Nootaikok's hand as the room filled. Around was what Nootaikok had taken to calling his "posse": Brett, James, Chen, and several other students who all lived on their floor. Those who had, by and large, rallied around Amaruq when the attack happened.

In the end, all of the blood-sucking vampires had either died or surrendered. But they hadn't been the ones raping the female students. No, three of them had been busy drinking the blood of a wolf Amaruq didn't know well. The grand Fae, who had done the raping, were all dead. This included Amaruq's attacker, who hadn't been killed by Amaruq or Nootaikok but by James and Chen working together.

He was more than a little uncomfortable with all of his fellow victims around him but he knew that was mostly because he hated thinking of himself as a victim. He tightened his grip on his lover's hand and thanked all that was good that Nootaikok was still his lover. They'd even managed to make love once, although it had been oral sex because Amaruq just wasn't ready for someone to be inside him again.

"Stop those negative thoughts right now," Nootaikok whispered, his tone playful even as his eyes were serious. "You're a treasure." He paused. "My treasure."

Before Amaruq could respond, even as his heart swelled, the dean of the academy called everyone to order.

"There has been an unprecedented attack within our walls," she began. "Perpetrated, I'm sure you've heard by now, by members of the grand Fae and blood-dependent vampires. Our negotiations with one member of their group failed. We are still trying to figure out why they pushed it so long, considering the blood-dependent vampires lose much of their strength during the day.

"Both communities have decried this attack and sworn it was done without their knowledge. We will take them at their word." She smiled grimly. "But we will not forget. Even now, trackers are seeking out the truth."

Was it Amaruq's imagination or did she look right at Nootaikok?

"Here is what we do know," the dean went on. "The grand Fae have long been discontented with the way some humans abuse the earth and seas and air. They are not, by and large, terrorists, but they are a strong people with firmly held beliefs.

"The blood-dependent vampires have a terrible reputation that is largely undeserved." She paused. "For now, security will be increased until we determine how they got in. Even the presence of a student among their number does not completely explain this."

Shortly thereafter, they were dismissed. Amaruq kept his hand in Nootaikok's as they left the dining room. He glanced around, saw most of his "posse" were staying with them, and smiled just a little. "You don't have to shadow me," he murmured.

Veronica, who was a dryad, answered, "I'm not shadowing you. I'm drawing on your strength."

It was said playfully but there was real pain in her eyes.

Amaruq dropped Nootaikok's hand and kissed her. "Maybe," he said before he could think better of it, "we should organize a survivors club." He didn't really want to sit with these people and talk about how horrible it had been. But he needed to do that, needed to help. He glanced at Nootaikok. "Open to everyone."

His lover kissed his cheek. "Sounds good to me."

Chapter Eight

In spite of the glorious weather they were leaving behind in DC and the equally glorious, if slightly chillier weather they were currently flying to in Alaska, Amaruq was conscious of leaden depression. Probably most of it had to do with how poor his sexual performance had been over the last couple of months. *But I can't exactly be blamed for that, can I?* No. Absolutely not. Not when every time he closed his eyes he saw the face of the grand Fae who'd raped him. Wearing a little reddish goatee and an unyielding expression, his attacker's face was superimposed over everything he tried to do sexually.

Of course, Nootaikok hadn't been pushing him at all. He'd been gentle and kind and supportive. And it wasn't like he was coming from a place of good memories either. They were both seeing therapists.

Amaruq thought he might actually love Nootaikok. Not the early love of hope borne of his dreams, but the real thing, made of mutual struggle, lust, and devotion. They'd grown closer and closer over the months since February, and even if they couldn't do more than occasionally masturbate in each other's company or, even more infrequently, have oral sex. Still, their emotional closeness had deepened and strengthened until Amaruq couldn't imagine being away from Nootaikok for months.

That was why they were taking this trip together and he wasn't going home to Buffalo to be with his pack. Nootaikok had reserved a cabin for them. And they weren't going anywhere near Anchorage.

"What are you thinking about?" Nootaikok murmured, taking Amaruq's hand and squeezing it lightly. "You're wearing a deep frown and your hands were balled into fists. This is supposed to be a vacation."

Amaruq glanced to his right, but the person in the aisle seat was asleep. Still, he leaned close and whispered, "I hate it that I can't have sex with you."

Nootaikok lifted Amaruq's hand to his lips. But instead of kissing it, he licked it gently, his tongue making small patterns on the back. Then he blew across the wetness, making Amaruq shiver. And making him unexpectedly dewy between his legs.

"I've been thinking about that. If you can be silent, I think we can work this out." And he pulled his backpack out from under the seat in front of him and settled it on his lap. "Put your coat over your legs."

Confused -- what exactly could they do sitting on an airplane? -- Amaruq obeyed. Keeping his hand in Nootaikok's he closed his eyes and leaned back against the seat, which wasn't comfortable, but was better than sitting bolt upright, the way he had been before.

"Open your mind to me."

This was something they'd been practicing. Amaruq loved having access to his lover's thoughts, especially when Nootaikok was overjoyed or distressed. Overjoyed was somewhat obvious, but the distress... That was different. Amaruq supposed he liked it because he felt less alone when he felt Nootaikok's anxiety.

So, now he opened his mind and at once felt the warmth of his lover's regard. *What do you have in mind?* he asked silently.

I want to make love to you. But it's going to require you to be silent while I pleasure you.

But... but we're on an airplane. There isn't room for both of us in the bathroom.

Nootaikok chuckled, both in their connection and

aloud. "Haven't you ever heard of telepathic sex?"

Amaruq had, although he thought it was almost impossible for mere empaths. Then again, talking mind to mind was supposed to be impossible for all but true telepaths, also. He'd learned from his therapist that the trust he and Nootaikok had built might have something to do with how they were able to talk silently.

Is that something like phone sex? Amaruq asked dubiously and silently. *I don't think you can talk me into an orgasm. Especially not with some guy sitting next to me, snoring.*

Telepathic sex is a great deal more like actual sex because we can encourage our bodies to feel how we want.

Amaruq felt his cheeks grow hot. *If that's true then you definitely can't have telepathic sex right now. Your jeans would be all sticky.*

I'm not too worried about that. I put a condom on earlier.

Amaruq turned his head and stared right into Nootaikok's eyes. "Really?"

His lover chuckled. "So, if you don't mind being slightly wet…"

Amaruq thought, *He's serious. He really means to make me come right here in 14B.*

Nootaikok squeezed his hand. "If you want, go to the bathroom. Then you won't be as embarrassed."

Amaruq decided this would be helpful. He shook the gentleman beside him, slipped down the aisle and into the bathroom, then pulled down his pants. Nootaikok's voice was in his head.

While you have your pants down, take a moment to stroke your clit.

Amaruq opened his mouth to protest, remembered where he was, and closed it again.

Nootaikok cut him off, not with speech but with an image: Nootaikok licking the inside of Amaruq's thigh.

Amaruq shuddered, and gently pinched his clit. He expected the image of the one who'd raped him to come swimming up out of the blackness as it often did, but instead, he felt more of Nootaikok's dark-haired head bobbing as he teased Amaruq's labia.

Come back to your seat, lover.

Amaruq zipped up his jeans and returned to his seat. Nootaikok was wearing a pleased, but not too lascivious, smile.

When Amaruq sat down, Nootaikok took his hand and placed it on his thigh. High up, but not quite on his crotch. Then he turned his head and softly kissed Amaruq's mouth. "You're wonderful. Handsome beyond words. Close your eyes and rest. We won't be landing for at least two hours."

"You were expecting to have telepathic sex with me. Here. What if I had said no? I mean, I haven't been able to get more than lightly aroused since…"

"I'm going to bypass most of your fears so I can replace some of your bad memories with good ones."

"I don't think it works like that." But then a precognitive vision took Amaruq, and he was silent for several minutes as it played out. He was in some city, he didn't know where, and it was winter, or at least there was snow on the ground. Three human-looking children were tumbling about in the white powder and hurling snowballs at hastily-constructed forts of the same. The children were all dark-haired and had skin tones like Amaruq. Or like Nootaikok.

In the vision, a hand took his and he glanced around, seeing Nootaikok smiling at him. There was some gray in the narwhal shifter's hair, but he was as handsome as ever. Dressed in plaid flannel, he looked homey and comfortable.

Amaruq rested his head on Nootaikok's shoulder in the vision. "Are you ready?" he murmured.

"Absolutely. Will Tilthos Charles watch our pups while we make the journey?" Then he smiled. "What am I saying? Of course he will."

Amaruq blinked, coming back to the surroundings of the plane. "What journey?" he whispered.

Nootaikok smiled a little. "Considering your undermind answered that… Just look for the truth."

Amaruq closed his eyes and searched. It came to him almost at once: Nootaikok was getting older. It was time to change him into a magical creature with long life, like Amaruq. So they would never be parted. "Who would change you?"

"Some dragon, I expect. Do you know any?" Then he laughed soundlessly. "James and Chen."

"Were those our pups?"

"What do you think?"

"I think we manage to get over my fear if we have three pups." Relief flooded Amaruq's veins and he relaxed against the seat. "This is one of the times I actually like being a precog." Then he thought to ask, "How did you see my vision?"

"It's sort of like telepathic sex. When we are both really open, it is possible. Knowing that future is coming, will you make love to me?"

Amaruq searched his feelings for the terror that had stalked his dreams. He sensed it wasn't too far away and yet it seemed less. Dispelled. "Okay."

Eyes closed, he saw Nootaikok slowly stripping. He was, indeed, wearing a condom, even in the imaginary world.

It's not imaginary, Nootaikok sent. *In a very real*

sense, I'm getting naked for you. He stood naked in front of Amaruq's eyes and began to stroke himself. *Tell me what you want.*

Amaruq didn't hesitate. His need had blossomed and all he could think about, all he could smell, was arousal. *I want you inside me.*

Imagine your clothes gone.

Amaruq tried but they stayed firmly in place.

Nootaikok laughed soundlessly. *That is an acquired skill.* In the space between their minds, he touched Amaruq's sweater and it was gone. So, too, were the tube top and undershirt that concealed his breasts. Nootaikok licked his way around Amaruq's left nipple before drawing the responsive nubbin of flesh between his lips.

Amaruq moaned, but silently, mindful of where his physical body was. He could feel the warmth between his legs and he touched himself in the psychic world, making his jeans and boots and everything else disappear. *I need you.*

Nootaikok laid him back on a bed that had magically appeared. He kissed his way down Amaruq's neck to his collarbone. Then he took the right nipple into his mouth. *Do you want to be on top?*

Amaruq nodded and they switched positions. When he was straddling Nootaikok's hips, he lifted himself and lowered gradually until Nootaikok was inside him fully. Then, locking eyes with his lover, he began to move.

It was glorious, the slipping in and out, the throbbing, and the sweet pressure of Nootaikok's fingers against his clit. He moaned again, keeping his mouth firmly shut.

Nootaikok pushed in, but gently, and they matched their pace together, undulating like one being.

Nootaikok's stroking of Amaruq's bud encouraged an orgasm to grow, to burst, and to wash over him. Over them both as Nootaikok's cock twitched and he came.

But he didn't stop stroking Amaruq's clit. He got a second, and even a third orgasm out of Amaruq.

Gradually, Amaruq came back to himself. His hand still rested on Nootaikok's thigh. His breath was a little faster, and he knew his underwear was decidedly damp. But he felt better than he had in months. He turned his head, meeting Nootaikok's eyes, and whispered, "I love you."

Horror shot through him. He hadn't meant to say that. It was a post coital blurting.

But Nootaikok touched the side of Amaruq's face and whispered, "I love you too."

* * *

Three days later, Amaruq rode in a kayak while Nootaikok swam through the freezing waters in his narwhal shape. There were half a dozen of the massive whales all around Amaruq, but he didn't have any trouble figuring out which one was Nootaikok. It was the one who stayed closest to the kayak and showed off the most.

He was having a tougher time reconciling Nootaikok's love for him and his ability to love himself. Despite the frequent therapist appointments, he still felt soiled. And he knew Nootaikok still had his demons to deal with. Of course, Nootaikok didn't need to go back into the field as a tracker unless he wanted to. Trackers were paid very well. So, that part of Nootaikok's future was settled because of the amount he'd earned before "retiring."

For Amaruq, he did want to become a negotiator. He hadn't dared lie to the grand Fae because he wasn't sure how much they could tell about lies. And based on what had happened back in February, he had a feeling he was meant to be one. But he didn't know where that left his and Nootaikok's relationship.

About an hour later, he stood on the beach with the kayak pulled up on the land and half a dozen Inupiat people standing around him. He'd watched them emerge naked from the sea and put on clothing that they'd hidden among some rocks. Nootaikok's clothing, of course, had been with Amaruq's things that he'd left on shore.

"These are my cousins," Nootaikok told him, taking Amaruq's hand. He introduced the half dozen men and women who could shift to narwhal and back. "This is my lover, Amaruq." He kissed Amaruq's cheek.

"You're all beautiful in the water," Amaruq told them. Then he blushed. "And you're handsome now."

Nootaikok's cousins laughed. Then they all took their leave.

"Let's go for a walk," Nootaikok suggested as he took Amaruq's hand and squeezed it. "I want to talk to you."

Amaruq's stomach knotted. "Okay."

They weren't twenty meters down the beach when Nootaikok said, "I wanted to tell you that I heard from Agent Weinberg's people."

The head of Public Relations was a force to be reckoned with, or so Amaruq had come to believe as he'd listened to his packmates who were in SearchLight talk.

"Basically, they said the blood-dependent vampires and grand Fae were sent, if not by their people, then by a subsection thereof. Their goal was apparently to prove that they could take the most well-guarded part of SearchLight."

"A terrorist attack, then." Amaruq felt cold.

"Yes. But Agent Weinberg's subordinates are convinced they can prevent another attack of the same." He sighed. "I'm not so sure, and so I've decided to become a tracker again and dedicate myself to finding out what subgroups violated our trust and why."

Amaruq squeezed Nootaikok's hand. "Please," he whispered. "Be careful."

His lover kissed him softly. "I will." He changed subjects, pulling Amaruq closer to his side. "I want you to know that I do love you. But I have the feeling you still don't love yourself. That's okay, for now. You were assaulted. And having the rapist dead may help your nightmares but it doesn't restore your self-worth.

"I want you to know that I'm not going anywhere. That I fully expect the vision you had to take place several years down the road."

Amaruq wasn't sure what to say, but a little of the burden he carried eased.

"I expect us to mate sometime in the next year," Nootaikok went on. "And while your family is invited, it's only if they can behave themselves. I will not stand by and let anyone abuse you. And surely your new pack will be present."

"How can you be so certain we'll be mated? What if I can't bring myself to a place of healing?"

"You will. You're strong. I have all the faith in the world in your ability to adapt."

Amaruq's heart swelled. "Really?"

"Absolutely." Nootaikok stopped walking, turned Amaruq toward him, and kissed his mouth.

Amaruq wrapped his arms tightly around his lover's neck. "You're wonderful," he murmured, echoing words Nootaikok had said to him often over the past few months. "I do love you."

Nootaikok's eyes twinkled. "Good. Because I have a feeling that after graduation you'll be carrying our children."

Amaruq closed his eyes and just held on while the world around him turned and seemed to come right.

Tainted Son (Wolf Schooled 2)
Emily Carrington

Biting is central to werewolf society, from discipline to lovemaking, but David is unable to tolerate this most important cultural sharing. When he falls for a wolf who longs to bite him, he must overcome his past or spend the rest of his life alone.

Liam is a werewolf with the ability to change his human guise. He's always been able to fool others... until he meets David, who not only sees who he really is but how he truly feels. But Liam has a deep craving, something he continually confuses with rage, and this just might drive David away.

Prologue

"If you cooperate, wolf, we won't kill anyone."

David had no trouble believing that the blood-sucking vampires, what his pack called mosquitoes, would freely murder. Some of the grand Fae, who were working with the mosquitoes, were already raping some of the female students, magic-born and human alike.

"You can't bite my neck," David said hopefully as he indicated the collar made of metal and leather that kept him from shifting to wolf or using his limited psychic powers.

The mosquito who'd pulled him aside grinned. "There are plenty of arteries."

David was surrounded by three mosquitoes, and they began to feed. One at a time, or surely he would have been sucked dry in minutes. But they seemed to be holding to their rumored stinginess, only giving him over reluctantly.

Terror was trying to take him. Biting was something, traditional or not among the wolves, that he loathed. Seeking a surcease, he turned his gaze away from the trio feeding from him... and found a grand Fae staring at him intently. David's lip lifted in a snarl and he met the other's gaze. And in moments, he was swept out of the room and into a nightmare place inside his own head.

* * *

David was playing with his blocks when the trouble started. Most werewolf children had blocks, the good, old-fashioned wooden ones that could really hurt if they were thrown or fell over on someone. But unlike the other pups in his pack, David didn't like to knock over his buildings. He enjoyed building whole cities. To that end, he had been given three sets of wooden blocks with animals on the first, numbers and letters on the second, and the third blank.

He was busy creating a town hall like the one in his own village when he heard the raised voices. One of them was his father.

Needing to see what was wrong, David abandoned his cityscape and crept toward the living room of the big pack house where he, his parents, and two dozen other werewolves lived. He moved quietly because his father and mother had been teaching him how to sneak up on prey. His father wasn't prey, but maybe the one he was arguing with could be. Especially if it was one of the wolves David didn't like.

He didn't like most of the pack. At least, he didn't like being alone with them. He was *different*, and although his mother was the same way and she wasn't picked on or singled out, he was. Having Fae blood mixed with his wolf nature was seen as weakness.

When he'd made his way to the living room and managed to hide behind a chair without drawing either of the adult wolves' attention, he prepared himself to attack. His father wasn't just facing anyone; he was facing the wolf immediately below him in rank. Gary was third in the pack. He always seemed to be causing problems for David's father.

Now, they were arguing again and their voices had dropped to near whispers, as if they were trying to avoid attracting anyone's attention. That didn't make sense to David since he, Gary, and his father were the only ones home right now.

Gary snarled, "If you had the decency given a gnat, you'd drop that dog you're sleeping with and that disgusting son of yours. They're Fae. Not worth anything."

David's lip curled. Here was someone else who didn't like what his mother was. What he was.

"Watch your mouth," his father said quietly. His eyes were narrowed and he was bent over slightly, as if he was preparing to change to his wolf guise.

Gary went on against the advice. "If you don't stand guard over them every minute, you'll come home some day and find them dead."

His father's change from human to wolf was instantaneous. He leaped at Gary, his jaws snapping.

David began to shift too, although more slowly because he was still a child and hadn't quite figured out how to make it happen on purpose. Gary shifted too, but unlike David's father, Gary's clothes ripped neatly, leaving him unencumbered by pants or shirt. David could see his father was stuck with both forelegs thrust through the sleeves of his shirt. He began to fight the clothing, but Gary was already upon him.

His change only three-quarters finished, David rushed across the room, shedding his shorts and T-shirt as he ran. He threw himself between the two wolves, snarling and snapping for Gary's throat. He managed to catch one of Gary's forelegs at the elbow. But then Gary dropped his head and yanked David off with his teeth. Instead of throwing David aside, as most wolves would have done, Gary dropped him at his feet and ripped into him with both teeth and claws.

There had never been such pain.

Then David's father was there, still tripping over his clothes. He tried to shield Gary with his own body. The next thing David knew, he was showered in blood. He blinked it out of his eyes and stared as Gary retreated several paces, snarling quietly.

Then David's father fell on top of him. His throat

had been torn out.

* * *

David came back to his eighteen-year-old self when he was dropped onto the floor. He fell to his knees and started retching as the memory of his father's blood raining down on him held sway. Dimly, he heard someone say, "It's almost dawn. That's enough."

"Maybe we can take him with us."

"No. Once we've established negotiations, you don't get your playthings anymore. Not you, not us. We've had our fun and proven that we're serious. There will be no killing."

David was dizzy. Probably from blood loss, he thought. He'd stopped retching and he knelt miserably on the floor while, above him, the mosquito who'd made the offer of compliance argued that they could drink a little more.

"No," someone answered. "We're not going to kill anyone unless they force us to do so."

Two of the captors seized David's arms and hauled him across the room, where he was dumped unceremoniously with the other students. David struggled to see clearly, but his vision was fogged. He tried to listen what was going on around him, but his ears seemed filled with cotton. He passed out.

Chapter One

Liam Abernathy volunteered at the medical clinic on the SearchLight Academy campus three days a week. He'd been given a special dispensation so that his required "work with humans" in his second year was modified. All students had to work with humans during their time at the academy, but Liam was allowed to serve magical creatures as well. This duty, however, was limited to six hours a week, and he'd discovered he really liked helping people. He was even considering changing his major from tracker or negotiator, to possibly medic. That would require extra schooling and he didn't really like that notion, being filled with restless energy to *do* something with his life, but the idea of helping people tempted him.

He would have probably decided to pursue a medical career already if it wasn't for his strange psychic ability. Patients and medics alike didn't appreciate not knowing who exactly they were talking to and Liam's ability to shift appearances was off-putting.

Today was Frost Thaw. This morning he had volunteered to work an extra shift because he hated this particular werewolf holiday. It happened every thirteenth of February, just a day before the humans' Valentine's Day, and in Liam's opinion it served an equal purpose. If you were mated to someone, it was a time to exchange gifts and get laid. For everyone else, it was a reminder of what they didn't have -- either never possessed -- or had had taken away.

For Liam, it was the latter. He'd moved to the US from England when he was nineteen. Two miserable years ago. His lover, who he'd met while the other werewolf was on holiday in London, had stayed with him a total of three months. Then he'd abandoned Liam. They hadn't made love, knowing this would mean instant mating under the old laws, and Liam should have taken that as a sign that they weren't meant to be together. Instead, he'd taken the resistance as the other werewolf's ability to hold himself in check and show good sense.

As it turned out, he was needed today. He couldn't quite get a sense of what had happened. The campus was locked down tighter than a drum and everyone was told, via text or over the computer in the case of employees, to stay where they were and not venture outside their buildings. If they were between buildings, they were to get to the security office as quickly as possible, where "your ID can be verified."

Liam had been working since six that morning. Shortly after sunrise, another text message came to everyone: *the threat has been neutralized.* Only that. Apparently, the higher-ups, who usually didn't bother to explain what was going on, were keeping to their pattern. Maybe half an hour later, the casualties started arriving. Most were brought in on gurneys, but there weren't enough of those and so wheelchairs were being used.

Assigned to comfort waiting victims or families of the same, Liam felt like he wasn't much use while every medic on duty and those who could be called went to work.

So, he was hanging around, trying to stay out of the way, when the last of the victims were brought in. All of these were ambulatory, shock in their eyes but not too much damage done to their bodies. They were arranged in three rows of chairs and told to wait. Many of those who had been so unceremoniously seated began to talk among themselves. Some were grumbling about being required to sit when there was nothing wrong with them. Others were venting about not being able to keep comforting the ones who *had* been hurt.

Liam approached, thinking to soothe their nerves. Instead, he caught the scent of blood and followed his nose to where another werewolf sat sandwiched between a dragon of some sort and someone who smelled half Fae. The werewolf's shirt was torn to expose one arm over the elbow joint. Like all the other walking victims, he'd been wearing something around his neck that left bruises.

Liam crouched in front of him. "Hi there," he murmured, catching the werewolf's gaze. "What's your name?"

"David Holstein." He looked away. "I'm fine." He flushed, probably because he'd realized Liam was a werewolf too and could smell a lie. "Not badly hurt."

That was true, but there were different kinds of hurt. "Where are you bleeding?" Liam asked quietly, because the inside of David's arm was bloody but not with fresh gore and Liam scented flowing blood.

David winced but didn't meet Liam's gaze again. "I'm…" He shut up.

"Let's go see where you're hurt." Liam's gut twisted. He'd smelled blood on some of the female students who were wheeled past. Had David also been raped?

David shook his head. "They don't need to see me. They have too many injured on their hands."

Liam stood. "I'll find someone to take a look at you."

But after fifteen minutes of moving from medic to medic, Liam couldn't find anyone. He'd said the wolf was bleeding, but was told that as long as it wasn't life-threatening, he could wait.

Security officers had started working their way through the seated students. Some were campus security, but some, distinguished mostly by their grimness, were trackers. Although "tracker" was a title Liam might hold someday, he was intimidated by the licensed killers. And yes, mandated murder was only a small part of what all trackers did. He knew that. He was uneasy just the same.

He approached David. A general miasma of fear was rising from the students, but Liam didn't know if that was because of whatever they'd just endured or if their feelings were being caused by the trackers. Some of them were holding hands and others were biting their lips. He crouched as he had before. "Okay," he murmured when he saw David looking at him. "So, I couldn't get anyone to take a look at your wounds. But I'm not done trying. I just wanted you to know I haven't forgotten you."

"What wounds?" asked a female to Liam's right.

He jumped, lost his balance, and plopped onto his rump. He winced, embarrassed, and looked up into serious, intense eyes. He hurriedly glanced away. "He was bleeding from a wound I couldn't see. But all of the medics have their hands full."

The intruder hunkered down. "Tell me what happened," she said, and her voice was soft. It sounded dangerous rather than soothing and Liam didn't blame David for shivering a little. David bit his lip, seemed about to speak, and then appeared to rethink it. He ended by saying nothing.

"You have nothing to be ashamed of," the tracker murmured.

Liam put his hand out and touched David's knotted fingers. "If you don't tell now, they'll find a way to make you explain later." Then, because that would probably be taken as a threat rather than as the encouragement he'd meant it to be, he added, "You did nothing wrong. This is the fault of those who attacked you."

Guilt lived in David's eyes when he stared at Liam. He apparently couldn't look at the tracker. "I was bitten. By three of the mosquitoes."

"The blood-dependent vampires," the tracker said, a note of admonishment in her voice.

"Yeah," David whispered.

"That's not your fault," the tracker said, but she sounded brisk rather than comforting. "We need to get you checked out. Especially since you're still bleeding."

"I'm not," David whispered.

"You are. It's barely a trickle, but you should have clotted by now. Stay here. I'll be right back." And she was up and gone.

Liam scrambled to his knees and grasped David's hand when the other werewolf showed signs that he wanted to get up and run. "Never run from a tracker. It's not good for your health. Besides," he said, aware that he was repeating himself because he wanted David to believe. "You did nothing wrong."

"Yes, I did. I tempted them."

That sounded so much like what Liam had been told some rape victims said that he felt sick. "You're not to blame," he said firmly. "They attacked. They were cruel. They broke the law. All you did was happen to be there when they snapped."

The tracker came back, but at first, Liam wasn't sure it was the same female werewolf. He stared at her as a medic quietly led David away. "You're like me," he breathed as he recognized the cloaking ability.

She glanced at him and her face softened just a

little. "Come with me."

They were allowed to step into an unoccupied office. The tracker shut the door. She handed him a card. He read "Marilyn Warner" and a phone number.

"Which part of England are you from, Liam?" she asked quietly.

He blinked. "How do you know my name?" Then: "It's because I'm able to change my appearance. You're just like the trackers back home."

"Trackers don't keep an eye on image changers, not unless they've done something wrong." She smiled. "I admit, I looked up your nametag in the archives."

Liam glanced down at himself, realized he was indeed wearing the plastic square that named him "Abernathy," and sighed. "And you did that because...?"

"Because image changers are my specialty. My counterparts across the pond have known about you since you turned thirteen."

Across the pond was a British term. "You're not British." Then he shook his head. He had nothing to base that on except her lack of an English accent. "Are you?"

"I dated an Englishwoman for a few decades." She smiled. "Long ago. I've lost the accent that I gained while I lived with her."

He wondered at her candid response and then realized she wasn't telling him anything that would cause her harm. She might come across as open and chatty, but she wasn't giving anything away. "I'm not using my power for evil or anything," he said, feeling defensive.

"You're still trying to decide how to use your ability, if at all."

Liam winced and then berated himself silently for revealing that weakness. "Do you follow all the LGBTQ werewolves around like they're kids playing with atomic bombs?"

"Just the very powerful magical creatures," she said. "And make no mistake, Liam Joshua Abernathy, your ability to appear as different people to everyone you meet is powerful magic."

He was swamped by the sudden need to know what she really looked like. "I'll show you mine if you show me yours."

She chuckled. "Why not? You already recognized me for what I am." And she let her glamour drop.

It wasn't exactly glamour because that was a Fae thing, the magic that allowed the Fae to look like one thing when they were alone and look human when they needed to. Neither was it anything like the human guise werewolves, dragons, and many other magical creatures took on. Those were alternate forms that could be worn like a different set of clothes. This was... well, undefined. Liam had never met anyone who could explain to him what precisely he could do and how it worked. All he knew could be summed up in three points. One, it was rare. Two, it was slightly different, depending on the werewolf. And three, some people feared his talent.

She was smaller in her true guise than he would have credited. So far, he hadn't learned how to add more than an inch or two to his height. Marilyn Warner looked Asian to his untrained eye. He'd confined himself to different European aspects because although the change gave him a great ear for accents, he still had to practice. Up until now, she'd looked like your basic Western European mutt. When she spoke, her voice didn't acquire an Asian accent. He stared at her.

"I can see you haven't tried half of what you're capable of," she said. "That's all right. You're young."

"Why don't you have an Asian accent?" he blurted.

To his surprise, she laughed. "Because this is my actual voice. I was raised by Japanese parents but that was two full centuries ago. I've had many years among the non-Japanese to grow into a new accent."

He blushed at being so rude. Then, remembering his promise, he dropped the guise he wore most of the time and showed her his true face. He was six feet tall with broad shoulders and reddish-brown hair that brushed his shoulders. His eyes were blue and his nose turned up just a little at the tip. He was freckled, densely so, and so he didn't tan. He'd ceased to worry about that, though, because he could change his face and body within the limits of his experience.

"You wear a much less striking disguise," Marilyn Warner noted. "I like that. It shows good sense." She frowned. "Now. We need to go talk to the young wolf you were trying to help."

David pulled out his courage and asked, "Maybe I should talk to him alone? He's been badly spooked." He didn't add that she was part of the reason, although not the root cause.

She took a small button off her coat and pinned it to his shirt collar. "There. Now I can hear what you do without being in the room."

He hesitated. He didn't really want to go in as a spy.

Maybe some of what he felt showed on his face because she said, "Tell him it's there if you want. He still may feel better without me in the room."

Liam nodded, accepting this. "All right. But I'm

not going to trick him into revealing more than he wants to."

But by the time they'd left their little conference and found where David had been moved to, they discovered he'd been given something to help him sleep. It turned out all the students with any sort of trauma had been given the same.

The medic assistant, John something, who'd shown them to David's room said, "You can stay with him if you want, Liam."

Marilyn pulled Liam back out into the hallway and shut the door, leaving David to sleep in the only occupied bed. Most of the other victims were females, so he couldn't share a room with them, and the only other males who had been hurt were a pair of lovers who, a medic told them, had made it apparent they wanted to be left to themselves.

Marilyn said, "I won't be leaving until we're sure."

"Sure of what?" Liam fought down a strong urge to protect David. That was ridiculous; he didn't even know the wolf. But David's pain had called to him. He wanted the wolf to be all right. And instinct told him having a tracker in his business wouldn't help David at all.

"That he isn't going to turn into a vampire," Marilyn said so softly Liam wasn't sure he'd heard her correctly.

Greatly daring, he grabbed her arm. She stiffened but didn't attack him. He forced his voice calm as he let go of her. "Is that a possibility?"

"Not very likely," she answered. "But there has never been an instance of a werewolf bitten by three vampires without suffering either some change in personality or appetites." She sighed. "I admit, I said 'turn into a vampire' to gauge your reaction, to see if you'd noticed him acting aggressive in any way."

"Nothing," Liam said defiantly.

Marilyn smiled. "You like him."

There was no reason he should but... "Yes. So?"

"And you don't like me much." She seemed unperturbed. She tapped the button on his collar. "Please keep that on. I don't want to have to interview him in his current state."

After she'd gone, Liam went back into the room. He pulled up a chair beside David's bed and set himself to watch over the werewolf. A little worm of unease wriggled into his thoughts as he sat, reminding him that a tracker must have a good reason to worry. But just now, David didn't look at all dangerous. He was like a puppy that someone -- that Liam -- needed to take care of.

* * *

When David came back to himself, it was with the knowledge that he'd basically been put to sleep. He didn't really like that anyone could have been doing tests on him while he was conked out.

He started to sit up, but realized there was an IV in his arm and that the other arm was restrained somehow. Panic clawed its way up his throat but before he could scream or do something equally "unmanly," he saw the werewolf who'd been trying to get his wound seen to sleeping in a chair by the bed. There was no reason to think it was the same wolf; this one was brown-haired where the other had been fair, and dark where the other had only been kissed by the sun. But he *was* the same wolf. It was like when David looked at a Fae, grand or lesser, and knew what they looked like under their glamour. It was also akin to knowing his own features: black hair, brown eyes like milk chocolate, a farmer's tan.

He blinked, and the other's aspect changed again, becoming reddish brown-haired with freckles all over his face. His nose had a funny little up-turn at the end and David smiled in spite of his restricted position. He'd heard about wolves like this one, who could change their appearance. They were supposed to be really rare. There were all sorts of legends built around werewolves who could hide their true face. Not the face of their beast but that of their born-with human guise. David wondered briefly why the other wolf's trick didn't work on him. He decided it must be a cousin to the magic used by the Fae.

The redheaded wolf opened his eyes and stretched. When he caught David watching him, he stilled. There was a breath of fear in his eyes.

David flinched.

The redhead blinked and his fear was replaced by concern. "Hello, ducks," he murmured in a crisp British accent. "How are you feeling?"

David didn't know what to say. He remembered the wolf's accent, vaguely, from before he'd been sent to sleep, but then it had been softened by something else. Could this wolf change the sound of his words as well as his appearance? That *was* some trick.

"I'm Liam Abernathy," the Brit went on.

Maybe not a Brit, David thought. But with some sort of ties to the land across the ocean. "David," he said after moment when he realized the other was waiting for some sort of response. Hadn't he given his name yesterday? Or, he amended as he glanced out the window, earlier today? It looked to be early afternoon and he didn't think he'd slept that long. "David Holstein."

"How are you feeling?" Liam repeated. There

was a hint of mischief in his eyes and David responded to that rather than the question.

"What's so funny?"

Liam blinked. Frowned. "I didn't think I'd shown... Well, I'm amused that I was nervous about you at first. You don't look like someone who's falling prey to a vampire's transforming bite."

David flinched.

Liam cursed quietly. "I'm sorry. That was... insensitive and rude. If I'm ever going to be a negotiator, I need to learn to censor what comes out of my mouth." He smiled a little, though without humor. "Same for being a tracker."

"You want to be a tracker?" Liam's ability to change his face and body would certainly come in handy in that case. David had never met someone who was *planning* to become a tracker. He'd expected, well, not that they sprang out of the ground but that they were made of people less... gentle... than Liam seemed to be. Natural-born killers.

"And now I've scared you more than you were." Liam sighed. "I'm sorry, ducks. I'm here as a comfort giver and I'm failing miserably."

His self-castigation soothed David's fear. "I guess my, uh, nervousness around trackers is ridiculous. Especially as you aren't one yet."

"Probably will never be," Liam said. "I've got to decide by the end of this semester what I want to do and I just can't make up my mind. But after meeting a tracker in action earlier this morning, I'm not sure I want to be like that. To have everyone afraid of me."

"That woman..." She'd been able to change her appearance like Liam. As some of the bards of legend could do, David didn't just "see" without effort, but he got a tickle that would let him know if a person's aspect wasn't their true self. "What's her name?"

"Agent Marilyn Warner."

"She's..." For some reason, he didn't want to draw attention to the fact that he could see through Liam's disguise. Not only did he offend and anger Fae who'd thought themselves camouflaged, but it seemed too invasive. David switched topics. "Thank you for staying with me. I'm assuming you're not a tech if you're still in school trying to decide between tracker and negotiator."

"I'm a volunteer," Liam agreed. "Now, for the third time: how do you feel?"

"Dirty," David blurted. He felt himself blush. He winced.

"Getting bitten by a vampire would probably do that to anyone." Liam shook his head. "That's wrong to say. Some people get great benefits from sharing their blood. Like the humans whose blood-based cancers or other diseases go into remission."

Apparently, David wasn't done spilling his guts because he snapped, "Yeah, well, I didn't ask to be fed upon. It's not my fault my blood is sweeter than that of other werewolves."

"I'm sure that's not --"

David grimaced. "It is true. My grandfather on my mother's side was Fae. It makes a unique blend that attracts vampires."

"You've been bitten before?"

"No, but..." David felt his cheeks grow even hotter. "But I'm an aberration." He made himself stop there. No one needed to know that he felt like a freak, that he was convinced the reason no one had ever wanted him sexually was because of his "uniqueness." *Or maybe it's because I'm terrified of being bitten. That's an aberration too.*

Someone knocked on the partially closed door and entered without waiting for a response. David shivered and huddled into himself as much as the restraints would allow.

"Is it really necessary to tie him down?" Liam demanded of the person who came in.

"While he slept, yes, in case he woke up afraid and convinced he needed to defend himself or flee." She came over and released the restraints. "Tell me your name, please."

David blinked at her. "Isn't my name on your chart?"

She smiled a little. It was a kind smile. "Yes, but we have to make sure you know who you are."

"David Samuel Holstein."

"How old are you?"

"Twenty-three."

"Who is the alpha of your home pack?"

"Pierell Gordon."

"What year is it?"

David told her.

Her smile grew. "All right, you're definitely tracking just fine. I'm glad to hear it. Now come the hard questions."

Liam stood. "I should leave."

David reached out and caught his hand. He wasn't sure why, but he felt... safe... in the other wolf's presence. "Please," he said when Liam looked down at him. "Stay."

Liam nodded. "All right, ducks." He sat back down. Then he turned his attention to the woman with the clipboard. "Please, Kari. Be as gentle as you can. He's been through a lot."

She nodded. "I promise. What's your psychic power, David?"

David darted a glance at Liam. "Um... I can see through Fae glamour."

"That's not a psychic power. At least it's not one I'm familiar with." She frowned. "It says here that you're an LGBTQ werewolf. All LGBTQ wolves have some kind of psychic ability."

"I'm an aberration there too," David whispered.

Liam squeezed his hand. "You're not an aberration. You're simply different. There's nothing wrong with you."

David shook his head but didn't protest aloud.

"All right," Kari said. "I have to ask the next few questions. I'm sorry if any of them hurt. How many vampires bit you?"

"Three." As the questioning went on, David settled into a simple call-and-response pattern. He held Liam's hand, feeling the warmth and support. When Liam started tracing little circles on the back of David's hand, David relished it.

But he was pretty sure his nightmares, which had been plaguing him since the day his father was killed, would only get worse from here on out.

Chapter Two

The library was almost unearthly quiet at this time of night. Too soon for the finals' crunch that always happened about two weeks before the semester break, it was ghostly at ten on this weekday evening. It had been a few days since the attack on the main student dorm, and life wasn't quite back to normal.

Liam prowled the library, moving between the shelves like the predator he was. His silent passage wasn't marked by anyone except the security officer by the front door who had seen him come in. Most of the security people were leery around him because he could look however he wanted to, and so they couldn't identify him by sight. But tonight, they were checking ID. When he'd handed over his ID, he'd given the security guard an apologetic smile and changed so he could see that Liam was the person in the bad photo. He didn't usually do that, but then, he didn't usually find himself in the heart of SearchLight just after an attack.

On his ID it said: "May not appear as pictured."

The security officer had studied him for a long time. "You have a dangerous ability," he said at last as he handed over the identification.

"I've been through all the psych evals," Liam promised. "Even the deep ones usually reserved for those found guilty. I am who the card says." He was a little grumpy about it, but not too much. The tensions on campus were still running high and he was sensitive to that.

Now, wandering around on the third floor in the guise of an African-American man of about thirty, he wondered if his understanding of the feelings around campus made him a better candidate for a negotiator for Werewolf Watch or a spy/information gatherer/mercenary.

He'd been chewing the question over since he joined SearchLight Academy. He had a limited amount of time to decide which path he would take. The general education requirements were the same for a tracker or a negotiator. As for being a medic, he'd put that aside for now. Surely his need to change aspects every few days would be off-putting to his patients. *And although I think my heart lies in the direction of helping people, I just can't imagine staying in school for an additional four to eight years.* At least he could make up his mind about that much.

Liam heard someone rhythmically cursing and the almost silent sound of cloth being gently hit. He crept to the end of the row he was in, peeked around the corner of the bookshelf, saw no one, and followed the sound. When he finally discovered who was making the noise, he froze.

It was David. He was holding a large beanbag chair off the floor and repeatedly punching it. This was one of three similarly made lounging chairs, the other two laying on the floor nearby in the little reading nook. The cords stood out on David's neck and his arms showed bunched muscle. He appeared to be restraining a tremendous amount of force. Which made sense, since he was a werewolf.

Liam read his posture and actions easily, as he'd been reading people for years. Being the son of an alpha gave him the privilege of learning how to read people. Both of his parents were excellent at knowing what others thought without having to probe their minds.

David was furious or deeply hurt about something. He was possessed of a need to get rid of some of his emotion, but he didn't dare do it where others might see him, which probably included his roommate because he wasn't in his dorm.

I should leave him to it. He hadn't seen David since the other wolf had left the hospital in the company of his parents, who had been sent for like those of the rape victims.

But David must have sensed him or scented him because he turned his head, his cheeks flushed, and said, "Hi, Liam."

That gave Liam a start. "How do you know it's me?" he blurted, too startled to deny it.

David let the beanbag chair drop to the floor. His face aflame with embarrassment, he said, "I just... I can see your true shape like I saw that tracker's."

His cover blown, Liam approached. "No matter what Kari said, that's got to be a psychic power. And apparently you can see more than the Fae in their true shape."

David nodded, looking embarrassed. "I wasn't sure if you'd told anyone that you can change, so I didn't want to expose you."

Liam shook his head. "It's no secret. That tracker? She can do it too, like you said. And she's been following me since I came to the States." He nodded toward the thoroughly beaten bag. "What did that do to piss you off?"

David grinned sheepishly. "Nothing. I just needed to burn off some energy."

He hesitated over that last word and Liam asked, "Do you mean anger?" Liam knew all about anger. It was more his enemy than his friend.

David scowled. "Damn you people, thinking you know so much."

"What group are you lumping me in with?"

Liam tried to make it a joke, smiling as he said it. But he was annoyed. And annoyance could quickly turn to fury. Being a powder keg *and* a weird sort of chameleon meant he'd had to work hard to get into SearchLight. At least, his father had always referred to his quick temper as something negative. To this day, Liam wasn't sure how much of that had been caused by chafing against his father's rule. Certainly, SearchLight hadn't found anything wrong with him or he would have never been allowed into the academy.

David's scowl intensified. "My roommate and all the other students who are whispering behind my back."

Liam knew the danger of rumors. That same monster had helped destroy his relationship with his lover. His anger dissipated. "That sucks. What are they saying?"

"That I'm angry because I'm acting like a mosqui -- vampire."

Liam wondered what made David change his word choice but decided not to ask. It was a good change, so far as Liam was concerned. "You did something violent?" he asked carefully.

David snorted. "I ripped a book in half. It was one of my own textbooks and I'll be replacing it tomorrow."

"And you… tore the text because your roommate accused you of turning into a vampire?"

David nodded, looking dejected. "And I proved there's something wrong by destroying the book. But I didn't want to punch him."

"Werewolves are just as prone to violence as vampires," Liam said.

David opened his mouth to reply. By the look on his face, he was going to snap or snarl. Then what

Liam had said got through because he shut his mouth, glanced down at his hands, at the beanbag, and back into Liam's face. "Then maybe I'm not turning into a vampire?"

"It takes humans being near death to turn into a vampire, and that's because their bodies lack the ability to fight off the magic. You were nowhere near death. And you're a werewolf. SearchLight doesn't know exactly how vampire bites affect other magical creatures, but it's a safe bet that since we resist other things like diseases and injuries, you're almost surely not becoming one of them."

David leaped forward. If Liam hadn't been prepared for some sort of quick movement since he'd seen the coiled rage or pain in the other wolf's movements, he wouldn't have been ready. As it was, he caught David before he could flee.

Except David hadn't apparently wanted to run. He wrapped his arms around Liam and kissed him. First on the cheek, then, with hardly a pause, square on the mouth.

A bolt of electricity ran through Liam, stiffening his spine and his cock. He groaned and pulled David to him. It had been long years since he'd been kissed, but this felt right.

Then David broke the kiss and Liam was thrown back into reality. "Thank you," David whispered. "I've felt so alone and lost." He pulled away and wiped his eyes with apparent impatience. "I'm sure you don't actually want a kiss, but I…" He trailed off. "You liked it?"

So, David could see more than Liam's actual shape. He could read the expressions on Liam's face as well even when Liam tried to hide it.

"Yeah," Liam gasped. "Yeah, I liked it." He tried

to pull himself together. "I… it's been a while."

"It's been *never* for me," David said, looking down at his shoes.

"You're twenty-three," Liam blurted. "Is your pack one of *those*?"

David's head snapped up. "One of what?" he demanded.

Liam was briefly intimidated, but his ire was up. "One of those packs that clings to the old ways, saying that LGBTQ wolves don't have any rights?"

David blinked, and the obvious surprise on his face was answer enough. "My pack has embraced Tilthos Charles's upholding of Firos William's rules. No," he added more softly, "no one's kissed me because I'm not wholly werewolf. My grandfather was Fae."

Liam remembered that. And he also reminded himself that "pureness" was important over here. Much more than it was in his own country, where blending the species was seen as a good thing if it made them stronger. True, that new point of view had only started to sweep through England thirty or so years ago, but it had been around longer than Liam had been alive.

"How old are you?" David asked.

"Twenty-one." He had a mad urge to tell David everything, from his ill-fated love affair to his growing love for most things American. He repressed it, saying instead, "Come to my room and spend the night. Tomorrow, you can go and ask for another roommate."

He was honest enough with himself to admit that if David's pack liked the new rules, that probably included sex no longer equaling instant mating.

* * *

Liam walked stiffly, conscious of the head of his

cock rubbing against his briefs. He didn't often care about which kind of underwear he wore, although he knew males, both human and wolf, who swore that commando was the only way to go. Now, leading David back toward his room, he was preoccupied with the friction. That he was aroused didn't surprise him; David was an attractive wolf with his black hair and eyes like wet earth after a spring rain. What did surprise him was the strength of his reaction.

He didn't have to mull it over for long before he realized its source. *He recognizes me. In any guise. I don't know how he does that, but it's a turn on. I can't hide who I am from him with only a thought. It's like… he can see into my soul.*

That was a bit of foolish claptrap, but he didn't push it away entirely. Ever since he'd turned thirteen, he'd been able to fool people. Even his own parents, although he tried not to deceive them. But when he'd first discovered his power, and for about two years afterward, controlling when and how he changed had been almost impossible. He'd had to stop pursuing education at a human school because of it.

Luckily his pack, one of three in London and the surrounding countryside, had several retired and otherwise former teachers among its numbers. He'd been ready for the exit exams by the time he was halfway through his seventeenth year. And, again because of their tutelage, he was prepared for the SearchLight Academy entrance exams.

They reached his room, which was on the second-to-top floor. He unlocked the door, knowing it was empty thanks to his werewolf hearing. He didn't know where his roommate was, but he wasn't too worried. He'd walked in on his roommate having sex more than once; it was time to turn the tables.

Only if David wants to. Don't forget; he's been through a terrible ordeal.

Liam glanced at David, saw the other wolf was biting his lip, and decided to ask him outright. He closed the door and said, "I want to have sex with you. But if you're not comfortable with that, or if there's some other objection you have, I don't mind you just sleeping here tonight. The important thing is to get you away from the person you share your room with."

David's eyes narrowed. He looked indescribably cute when he did that, like a puppy trying to be menacing. "Do you want to have sex with me because I said I'm a virgin? Or because you feel sorry for me because no one's ever kissed me? I will *not* accept a pity fuck."

Liam liked him very much for that announcement and he said as much. "No, I was worried because you were hurt recently."

"It wasn't rape."

"No, but there are different kinds..." Liam stopped himself. "Okay. If you're all right with it, I don't want to argue you out of it." He began by unzipping his coat. "There's a hook on the back of the closet door if you want to hang your jacket there." It hadn't been snowing, so neither of their coats was wet.

Liam stripped out of his winter garments. Being a werewolf, he didn't need much; the lightest of gloves took care of the abnormally cold temperatures. He tucked his gloves into his pockets... and stopped when he caught David staring at him. "What?" he asked, suddenly unnerved. The wolf's gaze was predatory.

"I like your hands." David closed the distance between them and took Liam's right hand. He lifted it up and kissed the palm. Then he traced a small circle just under the webbing between Liam's first and second finger.

The sensation was different than anything Liam had ever felt and he was moved to say, "I'm a virgin too," as tendrils of pleasure seemed to curl around his spine.

"You didn't kiss like a virgin," David said, his mouth still partially on Liam's skin. Then he drew back and smiled. "Although you blush like one."

Liam laughed ruefully. "I had a lover, but we never made it to sex." He hesitated but then added, "I like it that you can see who I really am. Is it like seeing something within one of those hidden pictures? Does it make you squint?"

"No. It's like your outer appearance melts away, running like water. For a second, it's not you. Then it is." He grinned. "Although you make one sexy as hell African American too. Just as hot as your Irish true self."

"I don't like all the freckles," Liam confessed. "I think they're... girly."

"Sexist bastard," David teased lightly. "I guess if I have a prejudice against vampires that you want me to get rid of, I can wait until you get over your issue with females."

Liam stared. "You *knew* I didn't like you saying mosquitoes? How could you?"

"It was all over your face. How could I miss it?"

"Most people do. I have a really good poker face."

"Not to me." David let go of Liam's right hand and gave his left one the same treatment.

Liam squirmed. In pleasure. "Where did you learn to do that? It's hot."

"I read it in a book once." David blushed, his tanned skin flushing pink on his cheeks and across his forehead. "I do a lot of reading. Mostly male/male romances."

He's been lonely. Liam knew that wasn't the only reason people read, or even the only reason they read romances, but he could feel the weight of loneliness on David's shoulders. It wasn't a psychic thing; anyone would have known it if they paid enough attention.

David backed up a couple of steps, took off his coat, and turned to hang it up. As he performed this simple task, he sang quietly, "Don't run out on your faith."

He had a very melodious voice, warm and baritone. Liam's skin tingled and he smiled to himself. He knew the original singer of that song, a human woman. It sounded just as heartwarming and uplifting coming out of David's mouth.

"You have a great singing voice," he offered when David turned.

"Thanks." He hesitated and then said, "I guess you'd better know this about me now: I've had very little in the way of companionship from other wolves. I sing to myself and talk to myself and just act like a fruitcake in general."

He wasn't actually embarrassed about his habits, Liam realized. "That's not why you blushed."

"Nope. I blushed because I try not to do it in public."

"I like you," Liam confessed. "Your honesty and your refusal to hide who you are. It's refreshing."

"Your… ex didn't show his true self?"

It was Liam's turn to blush. "Absolutely not. I didn't even know he was against SearchLight until after we broke up." That wasn't the worst of it, and he admitted, "I didn't know he was committed to the idea that LGBTQ wolves were second-class citizens until right near the end. He was bisexual, you see, and he decided early on that he would dally with male wolves but never have sex with them."

"Have his cake and eat it too," David murmured. He crossed to Liam and hugged him hard. "You didn't deserve to be anyone's second choice."

Liam hugged him back with one arm. With the fingers of the other hand, he raised David's chin until their mouths met. It was true -- David did kiss like a virgin. But he willingly surrendered when Liam nudged with his tongue. The heat between them climbed instantly from low to boiling when their mouths were open. Liam explored wantonly, loving the way David gave as good as he got, demanding entry after being submissive to Liam's touch.

Liam moaned softly when David cupped his ass with both hands through his jeans. In his true form, he had a little, round ass without much meat on it, but it wasn't as flat as that of most of the Irish Americans he'd seen. His muscular ass came from hours of running in his wolf form. He had quite a bit of muscle in his legs and arms too. He was pulled out of a consideration of what David thought of his ass when David lightly nipped his lower lip. Then the other wolf looked horrified.

"That's not a vampire thing, is it?" He started to back up.

Liam tightened his embrace. "Not at all. Werewolves do it all the time." And, as David relaxed against him again, he added, "Please don't keep looking for evidence of something that probably isn't going to happen. Almost surely isn't."

"But you were afraid of me when you first woke up in my hospital room."

"That's because... Well, I was asked to keep an

eye on you by the tracker who talked to you before. I was uncomfortable playing spy." He could see David's dubious expression. "Plus, I guess I was worried about you becoming a vampire at first, which proves that I'm prejudiced too." He flushed and rubbed the back of his neck under his hair. "But the medics let you go."

"Not until I promised to come in once a week for a checkup."

"Once a week isn't every day. If they were really worried about you changing, they would have kept you under observation."

"And I have to see a therapist twice a week."

"That's because you were attacked, not because they're afraid of or for you."

"How do you know?"

He wasn't sure at first. He shrugged. Then it came to him, and although it didn't seem to be substantial enough to share, he spoke it because it was the truth. "I have faith in SearchLight's medics. I have faith in *SearchLight*. Even though they've kept an eye on me since I was thirteen, they never bullied me or did anything unjustified."

"They followed you because you can change appearance?"

Liam nodded and saw David relax further. "You trust me?"

"You've had more direct contact with them than I have. The only experience I have with them was coming here and having the required medical exam and psychological evaluation six months before attending. And a few additional tests."

Liam read David's discomfort and thought to pursue it. But then David reached up and touched the side of Liam's face gently. "Can we kiss again?" the ebony-haired wolf asked.

They could and did, drifting to the bed as the kiss deepened. Liam pulled his T-shirt off over his head. David didn't hesitate, losing his T-shirt as well.

Liam was amused by their similar choice of clothing. "I think we both wear winter coats because it's the expected thing and not because we need to."

David smirked. "Just so." He touched Liam's nipples gently. "Are you sensitive here?"

Liam nodded.

David licked his lips. Then he bent forward and fixed his mouth around Liam's right nipple. His tongue moved expertly despite his lack of knowledge, and Liam wondered if this was also gained from books.

Moaning to show David he liked it, Liam brushed David's short hair away from the sides of his face. It was feathery and soft and he smiled at the feeling of it against his skin. David sucked lightly at the nipple he'd captured.

Liam groaned. "So good," he whispered as David started to draw back. "Please, do that again."

David repeated the motion and pinched Liam's other nipple. It was like having his cock stroked, Liam decided: utterly intoxicating. He tugged lightly at David's hair and smiled when David made a noise of pleasure.

They were sitting on the edge of the bed now. Liam nudged David back toward the wall and when David complied, Liam climbed on top of him. David stilled; his whole body went taut. Then he shoved desperately at Liam's shoulders. The scent of arousal was cancelled out by a stench of terror.

Liam rolled off, staggering a little as he tried to gain his balance. He stared into David's eyes and saw panic and terror warring for supremacy. He needed to show David he was no threat. So, nervous because he was putting himself in a vulnerable position but trusting his instincts, he dropped to his knees, tilted his head, and exposed his throat. He simultaneously brushed his curled fist down his nose: the werewolf sign of apology. And then he waited, remaining still after lowering his hand to his side.

David sprang off the bed and retreated toward the door. It was obvious he was terrified, but it was also apparent that he was trying to get himself under control. "I didn't... didn't know that was going to happen."

To Liam's surprise, David didn't apologize. Liam liked him for that.

"I guess the vampires' attack really got to me." He looked down and Liam followed his gaze. There, sticking up between Liam's thighs, clearly visible, was Liam's erection, which was only slowly reversing itself. It was easy to see because at some point either Liam or David had unzipped Liam's jeans. He wasn't sure who had done it, but if it comforted David now, he was grateful for the act.

"I like you too," David whispered, perhaps reacting to the sight of him. He stepped away from the door. "Maybe we can't do anything full-on physical, but I want to see you." He glanced down at himself and unzipped his own jeans. He wore bluish-pink underwear. The fact that he seemed totally unembarrassed gave Liam hope that his need to be cautious and not push hadn't been taken for resistance.

Rising slowly, Liam didn't approach. "You're brave," he said. "Their attack was unpardonable."

"I'm glad Amaruq and Nootaikok killed most of them." David laughed. "Well, a couple of them anyway. The others helped, but it was Amaruq and his lover who led the charge."

Liam was briefly distracted. He wanted to ask who those people were. But then he looked into David's eyes and saw what the other wolf needed. He crossed the room in three quick strides and took the slightly shorter wolf in his arms.

"Let's not think about death right now. May I kiss you?"

"If you still want to, after my panic."

Liam did and showed David his willingness. When they were hot and heavy again, he pulled back. "We need to both cool off."

"Or keep going," David said. "Just… masturbate together." His raised eyebrow turned that into a question.

Liam nodded. He wanted to jack off with this beautiful wolf watching him. "Condoms," he said. "So there's no mess for my roommate to complain about." He fetched them. "Have you ever put one of these on?"

David shook his head.

Liam grinned like the wolf he was. "Let me show you."

They both stripped down to their birthday suits, but only after Liam locked the door. "That won't stop my roommate, but it will slow him down, maybe give us a chance to cover ourselves." He gazed at David, who was paler where the sun hadn't touched. "I like a farmer's tan. It means you don't waste your time in a tanning booth but let the sun do her natural work."

David colored but said, "You're gorgeous too." He looked at the condoms in Liam's hand. "I have no idea how to use one."

Liam moved closer. "I'll touch you to put it on. Is that all right?"

David closed his eyes, frowned, and then

nodded. "What they did wasn't sexual. I think it will be all right."

Liam removed the rubber from its wrapper, pinched the end, and then rolled it onto David's hot flesh. "Oh, by all the gods," he breathed. "You're so beautiful." And when the condom was in place, he squeezed his hand around David's medium, stout length.

David's hips pistoned forward and he gasped. "Please," he whispered, "stop."

Liam did, feeling a little off balance.

"Not because I want you to," David said quickly, and Liam smelled the truth of those words, "but because I want to watch you touch yourself."

Liam nodded, reassured, and rolled his own condom into place. He locked eyes with David and began playing with his length. Almost at once, his ass ached for the dildo he usually used when stroking himself. He moaned and inched his fingers toward his asshole. Then he stopped, remembering that he wasn't alone.

"You like to be fingered?" David was pumping his fist, his eyes almost crossed in pleasure. "I can do that much for you." And he rounded Liam and spit in his hand.

Liam bent over the bed, resting his palms on its surface while keeping his arms unbent. He spread his legs and hoped. When David entered him with one finger, Liam spilled, crying out as quietly as he could manage, aware that other students might hear him. David chuckled, but it wasn't mocking. "I came too. Just from thinking about being inside you."

After he could think straight, Liam stripped off the rubber. He threw both of them in the trash and then hugged David to him. "We can do that anytime you want. And if we never get further…" He stopped, aware that he'd been about to lie.

"It's not enough," David answered, "but it's good for now."

"Yes. Yes, it is."

David rested his head against Liam's chest. "When you're recovered," he said, amusement in his voice, "let's go for dinner. Then, if it's okay, I'll sleep here."

"Will you be OK sleeping in my arms?"

"I don't know," David said honestly. "But it's got to be better than sleeping in the same place as my roommate."

"I like your truthfulness," Liam told him, kissing David's temple. "Let's go to dinner." He smiled down at their nudity. "After we get dressed, of course."

Chapter Three

David squirmed inside as his therapist, Dr. Jackson, nailed him with her gaze.

"I think," she said slowly, like a predator stalking a wounded deer, "that your fear of being bitten stems from something other than the attack by the blood-dependent vampires."

David couldn't lie to her; he gave her a half-truth instead. "That grand Fae, the one you have in custody, filled my head with visions that made the biting worse."

"Visions of what?" she asked quietly.

He grimaced. He would *not* tell her about his father's death. Or that he was responsible for that death. But unable to think of another half-truth, he sat in stony silence.

She switched tactics, but he had no doubt they would come back to this. "Several of my supervisors think having the students who were attacked help clean up the psychic mess would be therapeutic. What do you think?"

David considered his options, which included keeping his mouth shut. But when he realized he wasn't at all afraid of going back to the place he was attacked, he looked her in the eye and said as casually as possible, "That sounds helpful."

"Most of my other clients are terrified of returning to the scene of their pain."

David winced. He'd given her the wrong reaction. Damn it. "I guess…" But the cat was out of the bag now and he had no way to retrieve the slippery feline. "Look, Dr. Jackson, I've got something else wrong, but I've been coping with it for thirteen years. I'm fine."

"Something like... the death of a parent?"

David gaped. "Fucking SearchLight," he said with feeling.

She didn't smile or look offended at his profanity. "Everyone's lives are turned inside out. Including mine. It's part of your psychological evaluations."

David stared down at his knotted fingers. "Fine. If you need to hear it. I got my dad killed. And I was mauled by his attacker." That sound dramatic though, so he added, "It was only a few bites."

The faint and usually longed-for chime rang, announcing the end of the session.

David shoved his way out of the chair. "Thank you. I'll... see you next week?"

"A moment," Dr. Jackson said. She crossed to him and did something unprecedented; she touched his arm. "Your father's death was not your fault. Please use that as this week's affirmation."

Like hell I will. But he nodded without meeting her eyes and headed for the door.

* * *

Liam took a deep breath just before he stepped into the medical building that housed both the infirmary and the therapists' offices. He loved the smell of growing things.

It was the first week in March. Washington DC, where SearchLight Academy was located, was trying to decide if it was spring or winter. So, there would be days of seventy degrees and days of thirty. Days of sun and days of rain or even snow that usually melted when it landed.

It had been about two weeks since the attack on the campus. All of the perpetrators were dead except for two, a grand Fae and a blood-dependent vampire who had surrendered. So far as Liam had heard through the grapevine, the vampires and grand Fae alike were denying any involvement in a fringe group. Things were slowly returning to normal. Except there were definitely new "students" who weren't part of the regular complement. They were too cautious and paying too much attention to everything to be part of the campus. Liam wondered how long the extra surveillance would last.

He went up the stairs to the second floor, his mind more on the new "students" than perhaps it would have been at other times. For him, what they were doing could be his life. If he wanted it to be.

Tracker or negotiator? His packs, both the one he'd left in England and the one that had adopted him because a werewolf without a pack was either prey or dangerous, weren't helping him make up his mind.

The only asset he'd found was, bizarrely, Agent Warner. Marilyn, as she'd invited him to call her, was the only person he'd ever met who could shape appearance as he could. She understood the strangeness of sneaking up, unintentionally, on his parents when he was a teenager. She empathized with his worries about being a negotiator and having to choose one guise and stick to it. But she also seemed to get why he was cautious and nervous about becoming a tracker, for which his powers most suited him -- because his temperament didn't, and he wasn't sure which should prevail.

A good chunk of his mind was convinced that he should do what nature had made him for. The rest was convinced he'd be miserable.

Now, standing outside the therapist's office and waiting for David to emerge, Liam tried to put his concerns out of his mind. David would almost surely need to talk. He liked to discuss his therapy appointments.

Over the last fifteen days, they'd masturbated together several times, nearly three times a week. David relaxed more and more, and Liam found that he liked just spending time with the other wolf. Sexual attraction aside, David was fun to talk to. He'd read a lot, both American novels and British. He didn't particularly like history, but he picked up random facts about the past through what he read. He actually knew quite a bit about the British Isles' history from a historian turned novelist who wrote about bards and magic in a very historically accurate context. He might not know that bards were once real, and that their descendants still had some power, but everything he'd written about the human world had proven to be correct.

And, aside from the intellectual arguments they had about various books or historical events, there was David's laugh. It was a beautiful thing, at first self-conscious and then freer as he learned that Liam wasn't going to make fun of him.

Liam glanced right and left, saw no one in the hallway, and squeezed his crotch for a moment. He longed for David's touch. The black-haired wolf could certainly do talented things with one or two fingers.

His asshole tightened pleasantly.

The door across from him opened and Liam hastily dropped his hand back to his side and pulled down his T-shirt to cover the bulge. David stepped out. He'd been crying; the redness of his eyes attested to it. But he also looked calmer than he had in days. A good cry could do that.

Liam crossed to him and took his hands. Kissing the back of each one, he smiled into David's eyes.

"How are you?"

David searched his face. "Better than you, I think. What's wrong?"

Liam opened his mouth to lie, then stopped himself. Not just because David would be able to smell a lie, but because he didn't want to lie to the wolf who was quickly becoming his lover in more than just a sexual sense. "Not here," he said.

David nodded. He glanced back at his therapist, who stood in the doorway to watch them leave. "Thank you, Dr. Jackson."

She smiled, but it looked a little tired. "You're quite welcome. You're doing hard work, David. Have a great day." And she gently closed the door.

Hand in hand, they started down the hall. "Do you want to talk about your session?" Liam asked.

David shrugged. "She wants me to meet with several other people who were attacked and help to psychically clean the site where we were all held."

"That hasn't been done already?" Liam realized they had held the last all-dorm meeting in the main cafeteria. "Why are they waiting so long?"

"Apparently waiting for us, the victims, to be ready. It's a way to help us as well as the building." He shrugged again, and by that very gesture Liam knew he was disconcerted. "We'll be using sage and other astringent herbs."

Liam squeezed his hand. "Let's wait until we're back in your room." David's roommate had been counseled, and he no longer harassed David about turning into a vampire. It helped that David hadn't shown a single sign of changing.

They moved quickly through the halls, down the stairs, and out the door into the sunshine. For now, March had apparently decided it was spring. They went without jackets, having discussed their reasons for trying to disguise themselves as human. Let the actual humans appear human, they'd decided. To that end, they went about in T-shirts and jeans, enjoying the feel of the wind on their skin. And that wasn't just Liam assuming David liked it too. David had expressed his enjoyment.

They were halfway back to the main dormitory when David said softly, "I've been having nightmares."

Liam squeezed David's hand. "What about? The vampires?"

"No." Then: "Well, sort of. When they were biting me? This grand Fae conjured up... certain images... that I couldn't escape. Surrendering to the vampires was almost okay because I was doing it to keep others safe."

Liam stopped walking. "What?"

He must have sounded harsher than he intended because David looked away. "They told me if I let them feed they wouldn't kill anyone." He hesitated before rushing on. "But then this grand Fae, Erickson or something like that, put all this stuff in my head..."

Liam let go of David's hand so he could clench his fists. "Where is this Erickson now?"

"In custody."

Liam laughed bitterly. "Like that's going to be helpful? I've heard how soft SearchLight prisons are."

"They're rehabilitation centers," David said. "When you can live for centuries, life in prison is impractical."

"Maybe I could speed along his release from this world."

Liam meant it seriously, but David laughed a little. "That would be helpful." He caught one of

Liam's fists and smoothed it into a flat hand again. "Come on. Let's go back to my room."

They were almost back at the dormitory when David whispered, "I do wish the other students would leave me the fuck alone."

Liam pulled him to a halt once more.

David glanced around, though, and said, "Come on. This is something that shouldn't be discussed in the open air." He sighed. "I shouldn't have even brought it up but…"

"But it's bugging you."

"Only because they're harassing me about being bitten. About calling the vampires to me."

"Who exactly is harassing you?"

"Mostly this werewolf named Joseph, but…" David frowned. "I get that you want to protect me, but the look on your face when I came out of my therapy session… What's bothering you?"

Liam stared. "I was thinking about masturbating. There wasn't any look on my face."

"Your top expression was lust," David conceded, starting to walk again, "but your eyes held something… else."

Liam followed, struggling to regain his righteous anger. But David had neatly and effectively brought up what was bothering him and this was much harder to dismiss. "Maybe once we're in the room…"

Chapter Four

David lay with his head on Liam's chest. He wasn't going to fall asleep like this, even though they'd just masturbated together and logic said he should be sleepy. This was just so new, resting here beside Liam, sharing the same bed. David was too keyed up for darkness to take him.

He shut his eyes, and immediately saw the vampires' teeth. Longer than a werewolf's in human form, they were pristine white, seeming to glow. And, of course, just behind that image was the feel of his own blood running out of his torn flesh.

"Shh," Liam murmured as he rubbed David's back.

"I didn't even say anything," David protested but he eased under the gentle caress that nevertheless grounded him in the here and now. "Don't tell me you're a telepath as well as a shape-changer."

"Hardly." Liam chuckled. "But you got really tense. I'm guessing your body started to relax and that scared you?"

"No," David admitted. "I was thinking about the vampires." There was no way in hell he was going to admit to the other. No one knew about that -- well, no one but his therapist, and he was going to keep it that way.

Liam thumped him very lightly on the top of the head. "Stop that."

David snickered. "Yes, boss." But he didn't dare close his eyes. "Hey," he murmured, "Do you want to talk about whatever was bothering you earlier?"

Liam laughed. "I thought after sex was supposed to be a quiet time."

"Is that why you let me, um, almost seduce you?

Because you didn't want to talk?"

"Umm..." Liam chuckled again. "If you really want to know, it was..."

"Yes?"

"All right, so this is harder to talk about than I thought." Liam sighed. David's head lifted and dropped as the other wolf's chest rose and fell. "I want to be something in SearchLight. I've wanted to since I learned about their existence when I was a wolfling."

Teenage werewolves were called wolflings, just as children were called pups. The practice had arisen about the same time the word "teenagers" came into being, sometime in the 1920s. Up until then, those who weren't twenty were called pups and often resented it by the time they were finally given adult responsibilities. David dragged his mind out of the impromptu history lesson it was giving, aware that Liam had fallen silent. "And?" he urged.

"Well, I can't decide between being a negotiator and a tracker."

"Trackers are scary. You're not scary."

Liam laughed outright.

David eased against him a little more firmly, comforted by his mirth. "Why are you laughing at me?"

"Because that's almost exactly what I said to Agent Warner. Marilyn. What I did say was 'fucking creepy' and she asked me if I kissed my mother with that mouth."

David snickered again. "She sounds like someone I'd like," he admitted.

"What she told me is that trackers are just like everyone else, except some of them have seen too much and some of them see themselves as separate from society."

"Because they have a license to kill?"

"That too."

"There's more?"

"Yeah." Another sigh. "It's like this, Marilyn told me. Trackers have an extra two years in school because they need to learn out in the field if they really want to be trackers. Many die out there." He made a noise David couldn't interpret. "I'm more than a little intimidated by that news."

"If you weren't, you'd be crazy."

Another chuckle moved his head up and down. "Yeah, I guess that's true. I just... I don't know what I want to do, you know? I have this tremendous gift, or so Marilyn calls it. But it doesn't feel like a gift most of the time. I couldn't even control it for a few years. If Searchlight hadn't stepped in when I was thirteen, basically at the first sign of my 'gift', I would have probably ended up on their most wanted list. Not because I was trying to do anything wrong but because I kept getting myself into trouble. Especially with humans." He paused, and when he spoke again it sounded like an admission. "I get itchy skin when I'm in one form too long. Not literally, but that's what it feels like."

David tried to imagine not enjoying the skin he lived in. Then he cursed. Softly. "It's sort of like how I don't enjoy being in my skin sometimes. Especially when people accuse me of calling vampires. Or when my blood *does* call them."

A second thump to the top of his head. A little harder this time. "It wasn't your blood. They were just... cruel. Sadistic."

"That's not true. I was chosen out of all those students because I smell differently than they do."

"Does that knowledge, or conviction, help you

sleep at night?"

He actually sounded curious rather than mocking, so instead of snapping, which was what David felt like doing, he said quietly, "No. But it's the truth."

"Even if it is, dwelling on it won't make your life easier."

That was also true. "But everyone in my pack…"

"They know your blood is different? That's impossible. I've got a great nose -- well, at least a mediocre nose, and I can't smell any difference."

"It's not something they smell. My grandfather is a matter of pack record."

"So… your parent must get mocked too."

"She was when she was young, but now she's second in the pack. And our alpha never went in for mocking behavior."

"He tolerates it in others."

Liam sounded disapproving and David felt his familiar response: protectiveness. "He's not there to govern their thoughts and every action. He's there to protect them from each other in the stupid dominance fights and from humans' curiosity."

"Easy, easy," Liam soothed. "I didn't mean any offense. I just… I don't like the idea that anyone is hurting you. Even with the words they say."

A glow started in David's chest and spread all over his body. He sighed contentedly. Then he remembered they were supposed to be talking about Liam's trouble with making a choice. "Why do you want to be a tracker?"

"Mostly because I can do this." Under David's cheek, Liam's shape changed, taking up almost the whole bed by himself, pushing David to the very edge. "And this." He shrank to little more than a pencil neck geek. Then he returned to what David thought of as normal, although when he peeked, he saw Liam had given himself a beard and blond hair.

Liam asked, "Can you feel my beard or is that illusion to you?"

David got up on one elbow and kissed him. "I feel it," he said as he laid back down before his panic attack could really take effect. "But if I look at you, it vanishes. That's a pretty neat trick. But is that the only reason you want to be a tracker?"

"I'd make a lousy negotiator, slipping from form to form and never letting my audience get comfortable."

"But you're better at talking than, say, spying and hunting?"

"I... have a temper."

That was news to David. "Really?"

"Yeah." He shifted. "It's gotten me into trouble. When you mentioned your roommate? I wanted to pull his lungs out. With my little finger."

David wished he had a different psychic power -- telepathy, say, so he could know how Liam was feeling. So, lacking telepathy or its lesser cousin, empathy, he went with what Liam was saying. "You managed to control yourself when I told you about my roommate and about the other students who are harassing me."

Liam let out a breath in a huff. "Yeah, but you have no idea how much I had to twist myself into a pretzel to do it. And that's even with your preternatural ability to see what I'm thinking written all over my face."

"I was pretty upset the night you found me in the library," David admitted. "Probably I wouldn't have noticed unless you were spouting fire out of your ears." He considered letting the matter drop there but felt the tension still in the arm Liam had wrapped around his back. "How can I help you make your choice?"

Liam sighed. "I wish you could. My home pack and the one I belong to here in the States are pushing me both ways. Although the faction that wants me to be a negotiator largely just doesn't want me to be a tracker."

"Have you considered other avenues?"

Liam paused. "I've thought about being a medic. But if I'm furious all the time…"

"It seems to me you're only angry when there's something to be angry at." He hesitated before deciding to add something that might be offensive. "You could see a therapist about your anger?"

"Why don't you think that's a good idea?"

"I do, actually. But I wasn't sure how you'd take it. And besides, I just know the reaction of most wolves to being psychoanalyzed."

Liam laughed. "Isn't that the truth?" He stroked David's hair. "Thank you, but I'm pretty sure I'd scare whatever therapist I met with." He used his other hand to touch David's lips gently. "Will you kiss me? Then we can maybe play some more."

"Not unless we're on equal footing," David answered. He sat up, standing so Liam could get off the bed. "Maybe someday I'll be able to --"

Liam was up and kissing him before he could continue. When he drew back, he said, "Give yourself time and permission to take that time." Then he ran a hand down David's front, lingering between his legs until David's cock woke and pulsed with need. "I'll take the post by the door this time and you sit on my bed to play with yourself. I want your scent all over my sheets."

David shuddered with lust.

* * *

They'd masturbated again, their gazes locked. It had been as marvelous as all the other times, even if David wished he could get closer. But the threat of being bitten kept him at a distance. Now. David stood nervously outside Amaruq Jones's door. He was afraid to knock. Both David's therapist and Liam had suggested that he talk to some of the other victims. And because he thought he knew Amaruq best, and because he was another werewolf, and because he'd always been approachable before, here David was. He wasn't quite sure what he was expecting from Amaruq except more of the same balanced and gentle reassurance that he'd gotten before. He chewed his lip and then raised his hand to tap on the door.

He lowered his hand and chewed his lip some more.

"I'm sure he knows we're here," Liam stage whispered.

Embarrassed, David rapped harder than he'd intended. He scowled at Liam.

The door opened and Amaruq was there. Nootaikok, his boyfriend as well as his roommate, stood a few steps farther into the room.

David cleared his throat. "I... I need to talk. Want to talk."

"No, 'need' is appropriate," Amaruq said, his usually gentle expression tense. "Come in." And he stepped back, letting them enter. After the door was closed, he crossed to the desk in the corner and sat down.

That was one of the things David liked about Amaruq. He knew how to make himself less intimidating. Although he wasn't exactly threatening normally. Just... today. *It's only because I feel threatened.*

Nootaikok sat on the bed nearest the chair Amaruq had taken. He was close enough to touch his boyfriend, but he didn't do so.

David bit his lip and then left off it. "I... My therapist suggested... Liam thought..."

Liam made an amused sound. "It's not too difficult. David wants to know if he can talk about what happened to him. With the vampires."

Amaruq was out of the chair so fast it knocked against the wall. He clutched Nootaikok's hand.

Okay, so that's a no. David retreated quickly. "I didn't mean... I'm sorry." He felt awful.

Nootaikok had his boyfriend in a tight embrace. He said over Amaruq's head, "Maybe later." But he was looking at David and he frowned. "It's not really the vampires that you're concerned about though, is it? It's something else."

Amaruq turned in the circle of Nootaikok's arms and he looked calmer as if being held reassured him. "It's the rumors."

It wasn't the rumors, but David wouldn't share his past with anyone. Ever.

Amaruq shook his head. "I should have realized and sought you out. I just thought... I hoped you weren't hearing them."

Liam was suddenly at David's side and his hand was warm and supportive on David's back just above his jeans.

David nodded. "My roommate..."

"I heard about that." Amaruq wriggled free of Nootaikok's arms. "Didn't he apologize? I heard that he did."

"It's not really Keith," David admitted, the

words pulled out of him by Amaruq's understanding expression and compassionate eyes. Coming here might have actually been the right thing to do. But he still couldn't quite confess. Who had ever heard of a werewolf being afraid of being bitten? "There are at least a half dozen who won't leave me alone. Every time I pass... they whisper about me."

"Bastards," Liam said with feeling.

Amaruq nodded. He'd apparently lost some of his bravado because he retreated into his boyfriend's embrace once more. "You need to confront them. SearchLight policy is not to tolerate bullying, but some idiots don't realize their harassment is anything more than curiosity."

Nootaikok supplied, "They want to ask you questions but don't quite have the guts. Mostly because they know those questions are founded on little to no information. But instead of dealing with it in an adult fashion, they're acting like wolflings." He shook his head. "Even magical creatures aren't immune to immaturity no matter that they passed the psych evals to get in here."

Nootaikok said, "If it helps, take Liam. He'll make sure they toe the line." He grinned. "I see the mark of an alpha on him."

Liam bristled; David saw this out of the corner of his eye.

"I'm no alpha. My father's the alpha of London, but I'm no alpha."

"Then why take such offense?" Amaruq asked gently.

David took Liam's hand. "Come on." He didn't want to cause Amaruq any more distress, but he also didn't want to see Liam blow up. He had yet to see the other wolf's anger that Liam had spoken of, but he didn't want it to spill onto Amaruq and Nootaikok, who were only trying to help.

"How does he know about me?" Liam asked.

And even though it seemed he was talking to himself, David answered because he was amused. "How do Amaruq or Nootaikok know anything? Both of them are in their thirties. They have magic powers equal to their age."

They were standing by a window. David looked out across the campus toward the student union.

Liam came up behind him and took his hand. "So. Who do we set straight first?"

David smirked even though the thought of confronting anyone chilled his blood. He couldn't help what he was, but he was different. Deformed, in a way. And, just possibly, not being reminded of his cowardice on a daily basis would help him cope. Of course, there was nothing to be done about the nightmares or the memories of the way his father's blood had pattered down on him like rain. He repressed a shudder. "Probably we should face the worst of them first. It'll get easier after dealing with Joseph."

"Do you think he's in his room?"

David shrugged. "All we can do is check."

Liam squeezed David's fingers. "Let's do this."

David resisted the urge to hang back. They walked down the hall. He knew where most of the people on the floor lived just by the scent that hung around their doors. He knew Joseph's scent just fine even though he didn't want to and certainly didn't spend more time with the werewolf than he needed to.

He steeled himself because he heard movement inside. Then he knocked.

Joseph's roommate, Chris, opened the door.

"What do you want?" he asked, sort of rudely but sort of not, as if he answered everyone that way and meant no malice.

"To talk to Joseph," David said after unsticking his throat with a cough. He could see the offending wolf farther in the room.

Joseph got up. "Fuck do *you* want, halfie?"

Liam bristled.

David stepped between them to keep Liam from acting. "That's a derogatory term," he said. "You shouldn't use it."

Joseph snorted.

Chris, who'd retreated into the room, said, "He's got a point, Joseph. Let a prof catch you talking like that and you're probably out on your ear."

Joseph snarled. "Back off, Chrissy."

"Aw, blow it out your ass." He sat down and began working in a book.

Joseph returned his attention to David. "You're a halfbreed loser. There. No derogatory terms." Then he was reeling backward, his hands pressed to his gushing nose.

David stared, and then glanced at Liam because that bloody nose had to come from somewhere.

Liam kissed his blood-smeared knuckles. "Want another, *Joe*?"

Calling a werewolf by anything other than his full name was a terrible insult.

Joseph glared, but his hands were still pressed to his nose. Then, as his nose dried up, healed quickly like all werewolves' injuries, he started forward.

David grabbed the door handle and slammed the door, shutting himself and Liam out in the hallway. "Come on." He seized Liam's hand and yanked him into motion. "Quick."

"Next one?" Liam asked, sounding both cheerful and furious.

"I'm not telling you about anyone else."

The door opened behind them.

David yanked Liam around the corner. "Back to my room. And no more punching people." He dropped his voice. "Don't you know that people who fuck up and use violence here are expelled?"

"It might be worth it if --"

"Bite your fucking tongue." When they were in David's room, he locked the door and positioned himself between it and Liam. "Sit down. And calm down. You're not getting expelled. I won't let you do that to yourself."

Liam sighed melodramatically. "You take all the fun out of life." But now that the excitement was done, he looked sick. Or, more appropriately, disgusted with himself. "He deserved to bleed. You're not a halfie. And even if you were, he has no right to call you so."

But the sickness had grown on his face and David realized that now, after calming down a little, Liam didn't like how protective he'd gotten. That realization made David leave the door unguarded and sit on his bed beside the other wolf. "You really need to see a therapist."

"Why? Their suggestions suck."

David didn't point out that Liam had made the same suggestion, going to see Amaruq. He just held Liam's hand.

Chapter Five

David and about two dozen "victims" were in the windowless room on the top floor of the main dormitory. The room's floor was covered in a carpet. The color scheme all around was light brown, tan, and burgundy. The squares mixed with circles and triangles that decorated the carpet hid dirt and anything else. The blood had been taken care of, both magically and with mundane steam cleaners. David wondered how much of his own blood had been spilled here. Not much, he guessed. The vampires had let him bleed as they passed him around, but they also each had spent time licking him clean.

He shivered and returned his focus to the scrub brush he was using to permeate the carpet around the baseboards with a mixture of salt and sage. Cleansing magic would transform these simple elements into a spell that would erase any lingering magic.

It was something that could have been done by the maintenance staff, but David's therapist, and apparently other therapists as well, were encouraging those who had been involved to help rid the room of the last lingering vestiges of malice.

It was meditative. Or at least it was meant to be, based on the soft music playing in the background and the hushed tones everyone was using.

As he scrubbed, keeping his brush in time with the beat of the music, David admitted that it was actually helping. Not being able to smell the terror in the room helped. And feeling like he was restoring order made him feel even better.

With Liam's obvious interest in him, he'd allowed himself to forget for a few days that he was a cursed thing, doomed to feed vampires and be ignored by his own people as potential mate material. He didn't know where Liam had come upon his acceptance of those who were different from him, but he'd been grateful for it.

But this morning, getting the news that he was going to be doing something good to help reset the balance of the universe, David had been filled with a strange optimism. Strange, because he wasn't used to feeling hopeful about anything. But, he'd reasoned as he dressed before coming up here to work, if Liam had accepted him before, knowing what he was, who his grandfather was, maybe he could actually understand and forgive.

And, for the first time, David found himself wondering if Liam could be the single person in whom he confided. Maybe, he reasoned, if they were ever going to have real sex, he'd have to confess. Liam made it even seem possible that he could explain himself without shame.

He glanced to his right and watched Amaruq and Nootaikok working side by side. Amaruq had been raped once the grand Fae figured out he wasn't actually born male. Amaruq was staying close to his lover, and that last word, "lover", made David wonder how they managed to have sex after Amaruq was hurt so badly. Maybe they weren't. But whatever they were doing, their closeness couldn't be denied.

"Hey, mosquito whore," muttered someone.

David's hand faltered and he froze.

"Yeah, you heard me." It was Joseph again. Talking *sotto voce* and moving toward David with his own scrub brush. He was so quiet David didn't think anyone else heard him. Or maybe it wasn't his attempt at subterfuge. David knew from experience that being great at hearing didn't do a person any good if they weren't listening. And if his fellow students were as caught up in the cleansing ritual as he had been, they were inside their own heads.

"Go away," David whispered.

"Your guard isn't here to stop me, and you won't because you know it's true."

David wished he had a lover to protect him as Nootaikok and Amaruq were doing for each other.

Joseph moved even closer, his gaze trained on his work. He didn't say anything more right away, but his very presence was intimidating.

David knew he was less dominant than Joseph. Telling the other wolf to back off and actually having a hope in hell of being listened to was out. It also meant fighting physically was equally beyond his reach. If Joseph managed to catch David's gaze, David would have to back down. And he couldn't fight anyway, not unless he wanted to end up being expelled.

He was only a minority in the sense that he was a blended wolf. He had never thought his partially Fae status of anything but a curse, even when it gave him advantages here. It was like a small payment being made against an impossible debt.

"Are you thinking about how their mouths felt on your whore's skin?" Joseph whispered.

David stiffened, unable to stop himself.

"Yep, that's exactly what you're thinking." Joseph chuckled. He sounded genuinely amused. "You've been preparing for this your whole life and now that it's actually happened…"

David, unwilling to put his back to Joseph, moved even closer to the wall. He'd lost the beat of the music and he struggled to find it again.

Joseph tossed aside his scrub brush.

David tensed, unsure what the other wolf

intended.

Joseph crouched for a moment. Then he lunged, mouth open and eyes glinting.

* * *

When David came back to himself, he was laying on one of the couches. He knew it was one of those because he'd slept on this one a time or two in happier days.

He stank of sweat and terror. His hands shook as he remembered Joseph coming at him. He sat up, slamming his head against something. He panicked, drawing into himself and staring around with wide eyes.

"It's all right, David," murmured a voice he knew.

Liam?

No, it wasn't Liam. It was his therapist, speaking slowly and calmly as she rubbed her forehead.

"I'm sorry," he whispered.

"Not your fault," she answered. "I was leaning too close."

They'd bumped heads and David looked around quickly, afraid that he'd done other damage.

Two medics were across the room, tending someone.

"Who else did I hurt?" he whispered.

"You broke Joseph Tercerino's nose. His fault, of course. He was taunting you. Wasn't he?"

David winced. "Please don't expel me. I'll behave. I promise."

"You had a panic attack," she told him softly. "You're not responsible for that. No more than human soldiers with PTSD are responsible for their actions."

But even humans were put into hospitals and other places of confinement for their own safety and that of others. David pulled his knees up to his chest and hugged his legs close.

"Here, David," said a quiet voice. "It's your mother."

David looked at the security officer. The officer was holding out a cell phone. He took it with a shaky hand. "Hello?"

"Oh, honey," his mom said at once. "Are you all right?"

He'd called his mother when he was still in the clinic on campus. He'd needed to talk to someone he knew, and even though his alpha had always been understanding, it was from his mother that David drew strength. He was aware enough of other young adults, both human and werewolf, to know that wasn't the usual thing. Just one more reason he was different from everyone else.

"You defended yourself," his mother was saying. "I'm proud of you for that."

"Even if it might get me kicked out?" he whispered as misery rose to swallow him.

"You'll get extra help, not kicked out," she said with confidence.

"And if I can't be helped?" he asked, wincing at the fear in his voice.

"Then," said his mother gently, "you'll be welcomed home. Being a werewolf gives you lots of time to get over your fears and the terrible things that have been done to you. Although," she added, "maybe you would be happier with a less judgmental pack. We've already talked to Tilthos Charles. His pack would gladly take you."

David glanced around, realized he was looking for Amaruq, who was part of the alpha above all alphas' pack, and saw that he was alone except for the security officer and his therapist. Even the medic and Joseph were gone. "I don't want to come home, or go anywhere else," he said softly, almost whining. "I want to be here."

"Then we will find a way to protect you," his mother promised. "But if you change your mind, there's always a place for you."

"If I have another panic attack, I'll come home." Then, realizing that of course he would have another, David added, "Just to protect others from me."

After the phone was given back to the security officer, David laid his forehead on his knees and closed his eyes. "I guess I'm going home."

And no amount of soothing from his therapist could convince him otherwise. Because, sooner rather than later, he'd break again. His heart ached and he realized with a start that he didn't want to leave Liam as much as he didn't want to leave SearchLight. That was ridiculous of course. He hadn't even managed to have sex with Liam and surely they weren't in love. But he believed his feelings, and right now they were telling him he wanted to see Liam.

Not until I've calmed down a little. I do not want to break down in front of him. Again.

As if summoned by these thoughts, Liam appeared in the doorway. He rushed across to David. The security officer stopped him. But David reached out, his caution temporarily thrown to the wind as he was filled with longing. Liam took his hand and sat on the floor beside him. He said nothing, just held on.

Dr. Jackson, David's therapist, was talking softly and had been for some time. David finally paid attention and recognized that she was offering him a calming draught of magical something or other. He took the cup and drank.

The effect wasn't instantaneous, but by the time the security officer started questioning him to find out exactly what had happened, he was calm enough to answer. And although he did not tell about his childhood, he did explain about the grand Fae who had put visions in his head while he was feeding the vampires.

Chapter Six

David was determined to make the best of the last few days he would have at the academy. The thought of going home, retreating, was less than appealing, but he couldn't imagine moving to Tilthos Charles's pack either. The alpha above all alphas would surely discover that David's fear of being bitten was based in idiotic memories. Then David would be cast out and hunted down because lone wolves were always meted that treatment.

So, armed with the conviction that he wanted to know what love was like once in his life, David approached Liam's room and knocked.

Liam answered at once, his eyes flinty. "There's no chance of stopping me," he said. "Don't even try."

Stop you doing what? Instead of asking that question, David closed the distance and kissed Liam full on the mouth. He wrapped his arms around the slightly taller wolf's neck, stood on tiptoe, and claimed Liam as his own.

Liam groaned far back in his throat. He hugged David fiercely to him and they stumbled back together into the dorm room. David kicked the door closed. Fuck locking it. He needed Liam right now.

"Make love to me," he whispered before resuming the kiss.

Liam stopped him, putting a hand on the center of David's chest and pushing him back slightly. "You're afraid."

"No, I'm not."

"Okay, not now," Liam admitted, "but..."

David captured Liam's lips. When he was sure Liam wasn't going to protest right away, he drew back just a little and said, "I need you. Please."

* * *

Where was this coming from? Liam wasn't sure how to ask that question without sounding ungrateful for the gift he'd been given. He'd been nerving himself up to storm the jail where the grand Fae who'd attacked David's mind was being held. He'd been planning to catch the grand Fae outside, probably in the yard, kill him, and hopefully escape before anyone caught him. *Probably*, he thought coldly, *I wouldn't be able to get away.*

But that didn't matter. He needed to protect David. Even from his own demons.

He'd already taken care of Joseph, even if that wolf's ending wasn't as permanent as Liam could have liked. He was convinced that harassing David was no longer a good idea, and that was what Liam had wanted.

Now, here was David, distracting him and dominating their sexual play as he never had. Liam struggled for answers and had to nudge David back a step. "Aren't you afraid you'll panic?"

"I figured something out. If I'm on top, not necessarily inside you but controlling some of the action, or most of it, I probably will be okay. Can we at least try it?"

Liam saw the craving in David's eyes and gave in to what he himself needed. He loved David; he knew that now. He pulled this wolf, who was almost his lover despite their lack of full-on sex, against him and let David plunder his mouth. Surrendering to David was nothing like the times Liam had given in to his ex-lover, the one who'd never wanted to do more than kiss and tease. During those times, Liam had felt the need to control gnawing at his bones; he'd been desperate to guide the situation.

With David, it was soothing and exciting to give over charge of their lovemaking. He supposed that meant he trusted David farther than he'd ever trusted anyone in his life. David wouldn't deceive or hurt him and, just as important, David didn't want to dominate him. He would allow Liam to be alpha over him.

Alpha over him... Was that what Liam had been seeking all along? It sort of made sense; Liam's father was an alpha, a powerful one who ruled half of England. Alphas tended to beget alphas.

He cast the thought away. He wanted to keep David safe; let that be enough for now. He rededicated his mind and body to David's ministrations, only aware now that David was cupping his ass, squeezing now and then in a manner that was hypnotic and tantalizing. "You like my ass?" Liam whispered.

"Love it. I want to see it bare."

Liam stripped out of everything, hoping this would reveal David to him. Even though they'd seen each other many times, the sight was still provocative. He groaned softly when David traced a pattern over his own balls, not touching Liam now but still compelling him.

"I want you inside me," fell out of Liam's mouth.

David's eyes widened a little, but he smiled. Wolfishly, it was true. ""I've been dreaming of taking you," he admitted. Then he blushed. "I've never taken anyone before."

"We're both virgins," Liam said. "And that's all right." He considered David's narrow, not-too-long cock. "I think you'll fit well inside me."

"Lots of prep first," David said. "Do you have lube?"

Liam hunted it up, passed the tube over. "Please make sure it's warm before you..." It was his turn to blush.

"Can you lay on your stomach? Spread your legs?"

As he never had before, Liam trusted David wouldn't hurt him. He was prepared for it to be uncomfortable, for the possibility that he might even need to call it off before David was inside him, but he was confident in David's gentleness. "I've used a couple toys up there," he confessed.

"Do you have them with you?"

Liam nodded. "In the trunk at the foot of my bed. They're in a jeweled box." He laughed a trifle self-consciously. "I put them in a box like that so no one would be interested in them."

"Considering everything else in your trunk is traditionally masculine, that box actually draws attention to itself."

"I know, but I couldn't think of another way to hide my toys in plain sight."

David whistled. "This one's larger than I am."

Liam peeked. "Yeah, I've only managed that one a single time."

"Fingers first," David said decisively. He set the box next to Liam's hip and opened the lubricant. At once, the smells of vanilla and citrus, specifically lime, filled the room.

Liam relaxed, comforted by the familiar aroma. It had taken him months to find a combination of scents that reminded him of days at the beach when he was young without swamping him with memories of childhood.

David murmured, "You've played with lube before." He sounded intrigued. "Just let me know if I go too fast." And then, instead of pushing a probably chilly finger inside Liam, he kissed the skin available to his lips. He kissed it all over, lingering to suck here and there.

Liam shivered with need. He was a little embarrassed by the attention given to the place that sat on the loo to shit, but he was pleased at the same time.

And when the warm, wet finger entered him, it felt like an extension of the attention David had already been paying him.

Liam moaned. And, just in case David couldn't tell one noise from another, which was entirely possible because of their shared virginity, Liam said, "That feels good."

David moved that single digit around, setting off a spark of pleasure.

"Right there," Liam commanded.

David did it again.

Liam pressed his trapped cock against the bedsheets. "More fingers."

He realized he was giving all the directions, but if David minded, he said nothing. Wanting this to be equal, Liam asked, "Are you hard?"

For answer, David climbed onto the bed and lay on top of Liam, pressing the full length of his cock between Liam's ass cheeks. Then he sat up, probably on his heels, and pushed two fingers into Liam's ass.

Liam gasped, but more because he hadn't felt David withdraw his first finger than out of pain. Still... "I need a moment."

David gave it to him, tracing a pattern along Liam's spine with his free hand.

Gradually, Liam's body relaxed around the invasion that felt like a homecoming. "Three?" he asked.

David obliged him, moving his fingers so carefully that Liam began to get impatient. He rose up on his hands and knees and pushed his ass in David's direction. "Fuck me already." His member throbbed, and he was sure he was going to come any minute now. He did not want the shame of orgasming before he was even penetrated.

David pulled out his fingers and Liam felt the loss this time. "Please," he begged, "fuck me."

There was a terribly long pause during which David was surely coating his cock with lube. Then pressure... pressure... and David moaned, deep and loud.

"You're so tight." He stressed that last word as if he could hardly believe it.

Liam wanted to laugh, but he was afraid any extra stimulation would make him come. So, he concentrated on taking slow breaths. "Please," he whispered when he could talk without being afraid of upsetting the balance, "take me."

David did. He moved with gradual, firm strokes. His cock was slick and it moved in and out of Liam's body almost effortlessly. Except for the wonderful, wonderful friction.

Liam kept his ass in the air but put his face down in the pillow to muffle his cries.

David seemed to understand what he was doing because he kept his moans quiet. There was no need to announce to the entire floor what they were doing.

The pleasure began to build, much more swiftly than Liam wanted. He sucked in a breath and held it, desperate to hold off his orgasm. Then, because his body apparently had no intention of letting him dictate matters, he came. He clenched every muscle as the pleasure tore through him, leaving him exhausted.

He was afraid for a moment than David wouldn't come, mostly because he himself had done so very quickly. Then he felt a hot rush inside his ass and he knew David had also found his release.

They collapsed together. It was a sticky mess and they'd have to take care of it in a little while. For now, however, as David stretched out beside Liam, there was only one imperative. Mark David as his own. Liam turned his head, licked David's shoulder, and bit him.

David screamed.

* * *

Liam closed the door quietly, leaving David sleeping off the exhaustion of the brutalized. That turn of phrase made Liam shiver and grind his teeth as anguish and fury ran through him in equal measure. He slipped silently down the hallway while a plan of attack coalesced in his mind. He knew where he was headed, how to get there, and who'd he'd look like when he arrived.

He poked his head into the resident assistant's room. "Hi," he said softly, conscious that he was speaking more quietly than was strictly necessary but unable to make himself use a normal tone. "David Holstein is asleep in my room. He's exhausted and needs to be left alone if at all possible. He had another relapse." That didn't do David justice though, so Liam added, shamefaced, "I scared him. We were able to reach a calm place, but he needs rest."

The R. A. nodded sympathetically. "I'll make sure he isn't disturbed."

Liam made his escape. The moment he was alone in the stairwell, he bolted toward the outside. Memories of what had just happened in his room pushed at the present, demanding that he deal with them. So, instead of heading for the SearchLight Rehabilitation Center a few miles northwest of the campus, he found a sheltered place still inside the dormitory, undressed, folded his clothes neatly, and shifted to wolf. He used the door meant for werewolves in their lupine guise and fled onto the campus proper. He set his sights on the beginning of the long trail that circled the grounds and ran.

David had been trying to reclaim his right mind almost directly after screaming. He'd huddled against the wall but started talking. Babbling really. About bites and vampires, which he'd reverted to calling mosquitoes, and about grand Fae poking their noses in where they didn't belong.

He'd said, "Damn Fae, inventing shit and putting it in my head. As if my father would ever... as if I'd ever cower because of... Damn Fae. He was drinking my terror, or at least enjoying it on a less visceral level." Then he'd looked up at Liam and said, "I'd never be having panic attacks if it wasn't for that damn grand Fae. He filled my head with images when the vampires were feeding on me, tripling my fear."

Liam, his nose now up and scenting the air, growled. David had revealed part of this during his talk with the security officers, but he'd kept the depth of his reaction from them. Now, Liam believed he'd seen the full breadth of his lover's terror.

My lover, he thought protectively. *Mine.*

David was definitely his, and making love had only cemented the relationship, not made it. David had been Liam's, he now realized, since the day David picked him out in the library and knew him for who he was.

It was perhaps foolish; Liam wasn't alpha of a pack. He couldn't protect David that way. But maybe this was the way it was meant to be: find the mate, his heart's desire, first. Then go about building a pack.

His chest swelled with the idea of finding a pack

of his own and making David second in command of that pack. He knew the chances of finding a pack were low; there weren't just alpha-less packs running around. But he also knew that after a few more years, he'd be strong enough to find the pack he wanted and, under the laws of the North American werewolf community, take it for his own.

The only thing stopping David from accepting Liam's love, Liam decided, was this damn grand Fae who had killed David's hope. He headed back toward the dorm to collect his clothes. He knew exactly how he was going to handle this.

Chapter Seven

David awoke with a terrible headache. Probably from crying, he thought, as he rubbed his forehead and sat up, looking around for Liam. The other wolf wasn't there, and by the gradually fading scent of sex, he hadn't been there for at least two hours.

David groaned as he remembered everything he'd told Liam. He'd come so very close to confessing his terrible childhood trauma. That it *was* a trauma he knew, at least on an academic level. But he'd long ago vowed not to let it rule his life.

Yet, here he was, fresh from another panic attack and wanting desperately to go home. *Well, I will be. I promised my mother I'd be heading that way once I freaked out again.* But he didn't want to go home, to admit defeat.

He had something here, and even though it was centered around Liam, it wasn't all about Liam. It was about confronting Joseph. It was about scrubbing the windowless community space upstairs clean with his fellow students. And, yes, it was also about being listened to while he raved and not being judged. He'd seen the lack of judgment in Liam's eyes. And that very missing thing made David want to fall in love.

Maybe it's not about what I want, but what I already have. He wasn't quite ready to call Liam his mate, but by the moon goddess's mercy, he longed to declare they were together in some slightly lesser way for which werewolves had no words. The human word "boyfriend" was the closest he could come.

But Liam wasn't here.

Had he left because David was sleeping, or had he left in disgust? David tried that last word on for size and found it didn't fit the way Liam had been looking at him or the way Liam had, tentatively, kissed David's hand before leaving him to sleep.

He stood, thinking vaguely of going out and looking for Liam. He got dressed and opened the door... only to be overwhelmed by the scent of fury and uncontrollable anguish. It wasn't his. It lingered in the air like bad cologne. He followed it, leaving his door to close behind him. He trailed it to the R. A.'s room, confirming it was Liam's even as he traced the heavy aroma.

He knocked.

Dana poked her head out. "Hi, David," she said in mild surprise. "I didn't expect to see you for the rest of the day. Liam said you were sleeping."

So, Liam *had* been here. "I'm better now. Did he mention where he was going?"

Dana, who was human and so wouldn't smell Liam's emotional garbage, shook her head.

"Well," David said, trying not to show how uncomfortable and worried Liam's leavings made him, "I'll find him."

Dana reached out, touching his arm. "What's wrong?"

David swore silently. How had Liam, with all that boiling rage and anxiety managed to hide it from her and he, David, couldn't disguise a little nervousness? Instead of lying, which he might have been able to get away with, although he saw now that she was perceptive, he said, "I'm worried about him. We... things didn't end well after we..." He blushed and mumbled, "Made love."

"He was worried about you," Dana answered. "He asked me to make sure no one disturbed you." She smiled a little. "I put a spell around your door to make sure anyone who thought about knocking would come find me first."

David blinked, blurting, "But you're human."

"I'm also a witch." She chuckled. "Now, go on. Find your lover."

David smiled a little. "I will. Thanks, Dana."

"No worries." She closed the door.

David followed the scent, which was stronger and weaker in waves like a radio signal trying to get around a hill. He found where Liam had taken his clothes off, where the clothes had been sitting, and where Liam had put them back on. Since running around naked in human form was frowned upon, David decided Liam had changed to wolf and then back.

He left the dormitory by, he thought, the same door Liam had used. Once outside, he realized there were two trails to follow. He hesitated between them, unsure which was fresher. Then he saw a little rub of fur against the brick wall and knew Liam had gone that way in his lupine guise. The other trail led in the opposite direction. David went that way.

He arrived at the high security rehabilitation center about two hours later. It wouldn't have taken him that long except he'd lost the trail a couple of times due to the heavy volume of traffic. David thanked the goddess that Liam hadn't hopped a bus. His trail would have completely disappeared.

Once he realized where the scent was leading he slowed to a meander, frowning at the building about a block over. It was well guarded, and though he wasn't exactly a fugitive, he felt intimidated by a place protected by so many trackers and security officers of other types.

"David?"

He all but jumped out of his skin, spinning

around so fast he almost fell over. He gaped at the female who had appeared out of nowhere. There had been some people, humans, wandering the streets and taking no notice of the building housing dangerous magical creatures because that was how SearchLight wanted it. But this was a female wolf and she smelled vaguely familiar. Frowning, David stared at her until her form seemed to shimmer and resolidify. "Agent Warner," he said nervously. Probably it wasn't a good thing to let a tracker know that he could see through her disguise, but she'd scared him and he wanted to return the favor.

Unfortunately, she only smiled. "So, it's true. You can see through others' magical disguises."

"How did you know that? And how long have you known?"

"Suspected? For weeks. But I'm only just confirming now." She tapped a pin on her collar.

It was identical to the one Liam had been wearing off and on for the last couple of weeks. "You and Liam were spying on me?"

"I was spying on you. Once it's given an owner, my pins attach themselves to clothing without the wearer being in the know."

David was vastly relieved that Liam hadn't been spying on him. On the other hand... "What the fuck do you want? I'm not turning into a vampire. Isn't that why you were originally spying on me?"

"I see Liam has shared many of our discussions."

David scowled. "So, that's a yes. I'm *not* a vampire. Are you satisfied?"

"I was following him for his own sake, actually, and just happened to see you here, near where I tracked him."

David repressed a shiver but he couldn't resist

taking a step away from her. "You're a fucking stalker. Liam's not a threat to anyone. And what he chooses to do with his life is none of your business."

"I am here to make sure Liam doesn't get himself into trouble. His protective streak is, shall we say, legendary."

"Protective..." David's mind caught up with his mouth and he shut up. Liam's fury wasn't fury after all, was it? It was protectiveness. "He's an alpha wolf," he said softly, needing confirmation.

Which Agent Warner gave with a nod.

"So, he's..." David turned to look up at the imposing edifice. "He's gone to... protect me somehow. But what can that have to do with SearchLight cage 'em and treat 'em center?"

Agent Warner chuckled. "Aptly put."

David did his best to ignore her while he thought as quickly and as well as he could. "He punched Joseph. He bit me. But he was repentant of that immediately, whereas he still feels justified hitting my attacker." He was distracted for a moment. "Why wasn't he immediately expelled or put in one of those lesser rehab places for students who trespass?"

"He was spoken to, offered one more chance to keep a lid on his protective temper."

David nodded. "Because he's alpha material."

"No. We're actually stricter with those. Because..." She sighed. "His father is 'someone important.'"

David heard the air quotes. He let go of the questions that arose. "Why would he go into..." Then it hit him and he swore aloud. "He's going in because I told him that damn grand Fae planted thoughts in my head."

"Michael McCormick planted ideas in your

mind? Ones he created and not those he magnified that were of not of your own invention?"

"No, they're…" David started walking quickly away from her.

Agent Warner kept up, seemingly easily despite her shorter legs. "Yes?"

David hesitated. "You're not going to let me go in there unless I explain, are you?"

"Probably not."

He kept walking but slowed down so he'd have time to talk. "I was mauled when I was a kid." His stomach cramped and he clutched at it, halting there in the middle of the sidewalk. He felt like he was going to be sick. He'd said the words quickly, praying they'd get out without trouble. Apparently, he'd hoped in vain.

Agent Warner reached out to touch him. David flinched away. She dropped her hand to her side. "You were bitten. Several times. Nearly killed. By the savage bastard wolf who murdered your father."

David groaned. And then he puked. When he was done, he wiped the back of his hand across his mouth. "Yeah," he managed. "And I have to tell Liam the truth before he tries to hurt that damn grand Fae who only amplified the thoughts I was already having."

"I'll help you get in to see him. But you'll have to find him on your own."

David frowned at her in irritation as well as confusion. "Why the hell is that? You're a tracker. You can go fucking everywhere."

"Not into other trackers' territory. Not without a good reason. And if I make that reason known, they'll take Liam down. He'll never be allowed to accomplish the great things he's meant for. I can get you in as a visitor. Find him and talk sense into him." She removed the button from her collar and handed it over. Then she pulled it back to herself and adjusted something on its tiny back. "As long as you both wear these, no one will hear your conversation as long as you speak normally." She gestured at the mess on the sidewalk. "Do that and your cover's blown."

David took the pin and put it in place. "Thank you," he muttered, not quite looking at her. "I guess you're not all bad."

She smiled a little. "You should meet my son. *He's* scary."

* * *

Liam was in. He'd made it past the first barrier by deciding to go all out with his disguise. He'd altered his scent as well as what the genies called magical signature. He felt dizzy and giddy and just a little high as he walked down the halls behind a guard in the guise of another grand Fae coming to visit the one held here. He hadn't said if the other grand Fae was his son but had implied it; he'd increased his age, something else he'd never tried, and he'd deepened his voice to the point that he knew basso profound would be used to describe his vocal quality when he was sought after later on.

After he'd scared the shit out of the one who'd dared to violate *his* David.

He was stout and slightly bow-legged, auburn-haired and bearded. Only his eyes were the same color, and that was because he'd been exhausted after changing everything else. He would reach the grand Fae's cell soon, learn his name, and then find a way to make the other magical creature wish he'd been any other person.

Liam was only two doors away from the grand

Fae's cell now. His hands were balled into fists and he tried to hide the anger he felt as much as possible. He knew that one of his gifts of disguise was being able to hide most of his emotions from others, even their scent, but he didn't want to underestimate any guards here.

"Hey, Jackson," someone called from behind them. "This one's another one for visiting our resident academy hellraiser."

Liam glanced over his shoulder... and stared right into David's eyes. How the hell had he gotten here? What had possessed him? Maybe he wanted to see Liam take the bastard down? That was actually sort of hot, but David didn't belong here.

"I will be seeing him alone," he growled to his guard, apparently Jackson something.

And David walked right up to him, narrowing his eyes. "No," he said very quietly, "you won't be. *Liam*."

Neither guard reacted to his use of Liam's real name. In fact, the two of them were conferring conveniently off to one side. "What the hell --" David put a finger to Liam's lips. "It's not good to speak above a normal tone. They can't hear us if we speak normally." He touched the pin on his collar.

The one, Liam realized, that Agent Warner wore. "What the --" he began again, although this time more quietly.

David touched the pin on Liam's chest.

Liam gaped down at it. "That's not..." *Possible* was how he meant to finish that statement. But David was grinning, a little ruefully.

"That's what I thought too," he murmured, apparently reading what Liam hadn't said on his face. "But Agent Warner assured me..." He shrugged. "We're wasting valuable time. I don't know if these things have a time limit. The important thing is, you're not here to attack that grand Fae bastard."

Liam scowled, opened his mouth to roar, and shut it again. "I certainly am," he said in as regular a tone as he could manage.

"No, you're not."

"And you're stopping me… because?"

"Because he doesn't deserve whatever you're going to do to him. All he did was amplify… amplify…" David shuddered strongly.

Liam saw the terror in the other wolf's eyes and pulled him close. "Shh, shh," he soothed. "After I take care of him, I'll --"

"He didn't do anything to me."

"He planted thoughts in your head and made you insane with fear while the vampires fed upon you."

"He planted nothing. He only amplified what was…" He winced, covered his mouth, seemed on the point of retching, and then got it under control. He was staring right into Liam's eyes when he said, "He amplified what was already in my head. Because my father's killer mauled me when I was six."

And he turned, made a grotesque *urgh* sound, and threw up all over the floor.

Chapter Eight

Liam thought that late May was a good time to be in England. The flowers were all in bloom, the bees were buzzing contentedly, and the fog didn't come *every* single day.

Liam sat on a high, rough-hewn stone wall with David beside him. Below them, out in the fields beyond Liam's parents' homestead, sixty-plus wolves ran in the moonlight. David and Liam had been down with them a few minutes ago, and now sat on the wall, safely apart.

Contentment warmed Liam's bones like a fever. He'd grown so close to David it was impossible to imagine his life without his mate. Granted, they'd only been mated for about a week, united before Liam's pack, but the connection he felt…

They sat naked on the wall because getting away from the others as soon as possible had been more important than seeking out clothes. One of the pack had playfully nipped at David and panicked him. But David was calmer now

"I'm sorry he was an asshat," Liam apologized for at least the third time.

"I'm not," David said. "He got as good as he gave when you scared the shit out of him. I have *never* seen a wolf run that fast." He laughed, rocking back and forth on his precarious perch. Liam steadied him. "Overprotective alphaling," David said affectionately.

Liam smirked. "And you love it."

"That I do."

"Are you ready to go back down there?" Over the past months, with almost continual counseling and reassurance from Liam, David had begun the long process of healing from what happened to him as a child. Liam knew his mate still had a long way to go, but it was enough for now that David could endure and even enjoy soft nips as long as Liam didn't draw blood.

"I want some other kind of play." David grinned suggestively at Liam. "I saw a barn on your parents' property. Is there a soft place for us to lay and make love?"

They were off the wall and running, bare assed, across the short dooryard moments later. Liam guided David up the ladder into the hayloft where they found blankets as well as hay to cushion them.

They had no lube, but had tried several times in the course of their relationship without it. Copious amounts of spit worked almost as well.

Liam was on all fours in the hay, groaning as David entered him with first one finger and then another. "I want your cock," he grumbled when David pulled both digits out.

"In a minute. I've been meaning to try this."

And then David's tongue was between Liam ass cheeks. Liam cried out, not muffling his shout.

David laughed as he sat back and swatted Liam's ass. "It's not the most pleasant thing in the world, but if it produces that volume..." He leaned forward again and bit Liam gently on his right ass cheek, drawing no blood. "Are you ready for me?"

Liam nodded. "Always." He squeezed his eyes shut in an attempt to keep from coming right there and then as David entered him. He breathed in and out several times, measuring each to make it slower and yet slower. When he had some semblance of control, he whispered, "Please, David. Fuck me."

David rode him like the horniest stallion, his throbbing cock scraping Liam's secret place again and again. They screamed through their orgasms, Liam first, and then David.

And after they'd rested for about twenty minutes, they went at it again. This time, David rode Liam while Liam lay flat on his back. This changed the angle pleasantly and made Liam so dizzy with pleasure that he thought he'd never find his equilibrium while David was inside him. His cock ached and his balls tightened. He put all his considerable will into holding off and was rewarded when David came first.

"Fuck, but I love you," David whispered as they lay together in the hayloft.

Then he offered Liam his arm. "Go ahead. Draw blood. I want to see what happens."

Liam hesitated. "But…"

"Please?"

And because it was David asking and he could deny David nothing, Liam bit. David shuddered but after moment Liam realized it was with at least as much lust as fear. He grinned.

"All right, future tracker," David said, sitting up. "Let's go join the hunt before I want to tumble you again."

"And what's wrong with that?"

"Nothing. But I don't want them to think I'm too scared to come back."

Liam kissed him. "I'll protect your honor."

David smiled into the kiss and then nipped Liam's lower lip. "Maybe they can wait a little longer. One more time wouldn't hurt."

Outcast Son (Wolf Schooled 3)
Emily Carrington

Cast out of his pack for being psychic, Seiji seeks a home. Though he thinks of himself as lesser and doesn't believe anyone could ever want him, he still yearns for love.

Nicholas sees all of Seiji's potential, but he finds it difficult to be attracted to someone who's so lost. Will Nicholas' capacity for loving kindness help Seiji find himself and what his heart desires most?

Chapter One

Seiji Watanabe, not quite a member of the Issei werewolf pack, brushed his overly long black hair out of his eyes. He scanned the main SearchLight Academy notice board. Around him, the student union was mostly deserted. It was June 1st and the spring semester was nearly a month ended. Only those who had over-the-summer jobs or a summer class or two stayed. Seiji worked in the dining hall, keeping himself on campus through June and the beginning of July, waiting for his last chance at Werewelsh, which would start in the second week of July.

He didn't have anywhere else to go. If he didn't fail any more classes during the coming academic year, he would work in the dining hall next summer.

All right, he did have somewhere to go. The Issei pack would have taken him in if only because he was born of them. But given the choice between being little more than a slave or a potential member of SearchLight, he chose the latter.

He shook his head and his hair flopped back into his eyes. Now was not the time to think about what he didn't have. Scanning the board, he sought what he needed at that moment: a tutor for Werewelsh. Even though he was a werewolf, and even though most of the world's werewolves spoke Werewelsh, his own pack spoke nothing but Japanese and English. Japanese because that was where they were from, and English because their alpha, Issei Ryo, insisted they understand what might be spoken about them by the humans that surrounded them in the city where they lived.

Brightly colored flyers caught his attention first. One announced the Summer Solstice Dance, which was being held despite the dearth of students because many of those who had stayed considered the longest day of the year one of the top holidays. Another, printed on pink paper, offered tutors, but of the wrong sort.

He looked over the whole board and saw no Werewelsh tutors. Panic gnawed at his innards. If he failed the class again, he'd be out of SearchLight Academy. Something like a third of the students who joined the academy flunked out in the first year. Seiji had considered himself to be on the fast track to success... until bombing Professor Lepa's Intro to Werewelsh in the spring.

You have nowhere to go, a corner of his mind whispered.

More importantly, he told himself firmly, *I'd lose my chance to become a tracker.*

SearchLight's trackers were a combination of negotiator, hunter, spy, and, when necessary, executioner. They were the elite, the department rumored to be feared by all but the heads of SearchLight. *And maybe even the higher-ups fear trackers. Because if they're corrupt, they might be targeted for removal.*

If even SearchLight, rumored to be the most powerful organization in the world, largely feared trackers, their own people, then maybe as one of them Seiji would be safe from his alpha's wrath.

Someone approached the notice board, whistling off key.

Seiji glanced at the new arrival and saw he was taller and broader than Seiji himself, and that he was putting a piece of paper up on the board.

Want a Werewelsh tutor? Call Nicholas Black, campus extension x4857.

"Are you Nicholas?" Seiji asked, inhaling

discreetly to see if he was a werewolf also.

The other student nodded. "Looking for a tutor?"

"Desperately," Seiji confessed.

Nicholas raised a blond eyebrow. His eyes were green and seemed to be windows to a mischievous spirit. "I know you. We were in class during spring semester."

Seiji blinked, startled. "Um, I guess so. Which class?"

Nicholas laughed. "Werewelsh. I guess it was a bitch for you, huh?"

Nodding miserably, Seiji asked, "Can you really help me? And how much do you charge?"

"Five dollars an hour."

"Why so little?" Seiji blurted.

"Because I'm a sophomore and we're only allowed to ask for five bucks. When I'm a senior, I can charge a whole whopping fifteen." Nicholas snorted. "Something about keeping education affordable." Despite his words there was empathy in his gaze, as if he understood the need for an education-for-all policy.

Seiji thought about his job, which would end in late July so that he could concentrate on his second chance class. His work in the dining hall was far from glamorous, but it would allow him to pay Nicholas. "Well, I'm glad it's not too much. But I can pay you another couple of dollars under the table if you want."

Nicholas shook his head. "If my alpha found out, he'd tan my hide." He tilted his head a little and his eyes sparkled. "Are you always this honest?"

"Werewolves can't lie to each other," Seiji pointed out.

"Nope, but that doesn't mean you have to blurt out 'the whole truth and nothing but the truth, so help you moon goddess'." He paused before adding,

"Although I'd love to know something, and you might run at the mouth just enough to tell me. Why do you wear clothes at least two sizes too big?"

Seiji pulled at the hem of his T-shirt. "Um, none of your business?"

Nicholas grinned. "I like that better."

"Why were you in first year Werewelsh?" Seiji asked.

"I rearranged my schedule and took some second year stuff first."

Confused, Seiji asked, "Is that possible?"

"It is if you have a learning disability and courses heavy in reading are all required at the same time. So, instead of Werewelsh, I took 'Magical Creatures and Spatial Relations'."

"Isn't that the one where you find out all the personal space requirements for everything from wolves to humans?"

"That, and most of their tells when it comes to nonverbal communication." He smiled. "You'll probably enjoy that more than Werewelsh."

"If I pass the July/August class. We only get two chances."

Nicholas looked pensive, and Seiji wondered what he was going to ask. Maybe he would inquire as to how Seiji could fail a class that was offered in the first year, supposedly the easiest year.

Instead, when he spoke, the other wolf changed the subject.

"Let's go compare schedules." He pointed at a table that was usually taken over by seniors during the fall and spring semesters. "I have to work all day tomorrow, but we can set up for later in the week."

Seiji followed him over to the table, his gaze dropping to the slight roundness of Nicholas's ass.

That's what got you in trouble with Alpha Ryo in the first place. Stop it. If he'd been able to control his wandering eye, he wouldn't have been given a my-way-or-the-highway lecture. And a beating.

* * *

Nicholas was a grunt at the campus's main library. He did all the deliveries to departments, like trundling the projectors or VCRs around. Some of the newer rooms had LCD screens, but not everything had been upgraded. According to the head librarian, Mrs. Smythe-David, funding was being spent on more important things. Like books.

"It's always preferable to use things until they're no longer of use. And many of our volumes have been read to rags."

Nicholas tended to think that access to good technology was just as important as written knowledge, but he didn't dare argue with his boss. Being a grunt meant he could be fired out of hand if he roused any of his coworkers' ire.

Today, his mind was taken up with thoughts outside of work as he shelved tomes on this or that. He was thinking about Seiji. Even if the black haired werewolf with the Japanese features didn't remember him, Nicholas had watched *him* all semester. Not because Seiji was particularly outspoken in class, but because he was attractive. In a scruffy, clothes-too-big sort of way. His brown eyes were soulful and his small mouth was beautiful when he smiled.

Nicholas had slept with over half of the gay or bisexual males in his year. It was time to expand his circle. And maybe Seiji wasn't gay, or bi, but there was no harm in asking.

The best thing that ever happened to our world, he thought as he shelved *Magical Flora and Where to*

Find it, 23rd Edition, was Tilthos Charles taking over as alpha above all alphas. *LGBTQ and psychic wolves are equals with straight wolves now, and having sex with someone doesn't automatically mean you have to marry them.*

Of course, there were still those traditionalists who discriminated against LGBTQ wolves, and even more who still thought having fun in the bedroom should lead directly to mating for straight and nonstraight wolves alike, but Alpha Tilthos Charles was slowly changing attitudes.

His shelving done for awhile, Nicholas headed back toward the front desk. Doubtless someone would have something for him to do. He only hoped it wasn't cataloguing. That was boring, dusty work.

He passed one of the study carrels, glanced over... and stopped. Seiji was sitting there, poring over an open textbook. He kept rubbing at his forehead and there was a deep frown on his face.

"Do you work with flash cards?" Nicholas asked, thinking of a particularly arousing way to use the standard study tool.

Seiji jumped. He said something in another language that sounded like a curse because of the inflection he gave it. "You scared me," he said. Then: "I know. I know. Trackers are supposed to be ready all the time."

Nicholas blinked. "You want to be a tracker?"

Seiji flushed. "Yeah," he muttered.

Nicholas whistled. "That's aiming pretty high."

Seiji said defensively, "It's what I want to be." He glanced at Nicholas and seemed to rein in his ill mood. "What about you?"

"A negotiator for Werewolf Watch. Why do you want to be a tracker?"

Seiji shrugged. "What did you ask about flashcards?"

So. He can be circumspect about some things. "I was wondering if you use them."

"No."

Nicholas's cock seemed to leap to attention. He repressed a grin by reminding himself that Seiji might not even be gay. "I'll make you some if I get a chance. If not, we can start with that tomorrow. It'll be helpful," he added when he saw Seiji's doubtful expression.

"I can't remember anything even after I've just read it," Seiji said morosely.

"That's because you haven't turned it into a game yet." Nicholas winked. "We'll meet in my room, like we discussed. Ten still okay with you?"

Seiji nodded.

"And if you'll take one more piece of advice, lay off the book reading for now. All it's going to do is frustrate you."

Seiji hesitated. Then he closed the book slowly. "I guess I could give it a rest for a little while. Do you want me to make the flashcards?"

"Nope," Nicholas said as he came to a decision. "We'll do it tomorrow after I quiz you."

Seiji winced. "Why?"

"Why am I going to test your knowledge? So I know where you need help."

Seiji sighed and began packing up his text and notes. "I don't know anything."

Nicholas crossed to him and touched his shoulder. "One thing you can work on tonight," he said softly.

Seiji looked up hopefully

"Try some positive self-talk."

"Huh?"

"Stop calling yourself a failure in the back of your head."

Seiji looked startled. "It's that obvious?"

Nicholas nodded. Then he leaned close and kissed Seiji's cheek. It was a bold move, especially with his lack of knowledge, but he couldn't help himself. The shorter wolf looked so lost and vulnerable. "Do yourself some good. I can see you're going to worry all night long. Take a run."

"Around campus?" Seiji sounded like that didn't seem too exciting.

"How about just around the track?" Which was the only place, except the perimeter, where magical creatures were allowed to run in their true form. "Shift to your wolf and go for broke. See how fast you can go, and for how long." He kissed Seiji again because the other wolf hadn't pulled away. "I expect a full report in the morning."

Finally, Seiji was smiling. "Okay." And he returned Nicholas's kiss. But then he looked horrified. "That was just a thank you. Do *not* read too much into that."

Confused but also aroused, Nicholas tried to play it off. "Okay." He escaped. *What exactly is he playing at? If he's not gay, and his defensiveness about the kiss seems to mean that, then why did he do it? Then again, if he is straight, why did he let me peck him on the cheek?*

He had no answers, but he did know one thing: Seiji was beautiful, and the added thrill of not knowing his sexuality was a turn on.

As soon as I'm let off here, I'm going to go masturbate. Because if I don't, I might just try to jump him without buying him dinner.

He laughed quietly as he headed back toward

the main desk. He was one horny bastard and he knew it, but this was probably the first time he'd been sexually excited about a potentially straight person.

Chapter Two

Seiji was nervous as he approached Nicholas's room at nine fifty-five. It was two floors above his own, in the main dormitory at the academy. The whole edifice was eight floors high and had three wings in addition to the main structure. But what Seiji was really thinking about was the welter of emotions that had come rolling off Nicholas yesterday. Lust had been ascendant, but concern, caring, and plain old curiosity had followed on its heels.

Sometimes being a strong empath caused problems for him.

Seiji winced away from the truth of those emotions -- not because they were bad in and of themselves, but because of what they said about *him*. Being an empath in some packs was just fine, or so he'd heard. But being one in his birth pack meant slavery.

He'd heard about the new alpha above all alphas, supposedly a half werewolf who was gay and a phenomenal telepath. But Issei Ryo was... There weren't any appropriate words, at least not in Japanese or English, for how badly the alpha of the Issei pack treated his LGBTQ and psychic wolves.

Shouldering past that truth and promising himself that he would squelch his empathy as far down as it would go, Seiji knocked on Nicholas's door.

Nicholas was there, smiling at him. The emotions that flooded out of him were all about joy at seeing Seiji and anticipation about... something.

"Come on in. I see you brought your book."

"And some blank flashcards." He stepped in when Nicholas moved aside... and he was hit with the potent scent of arousal. The window was open and there was a fan on, probably to take care of the scent of need, but the air outside was still and the aroma clung to everything.

Nicholas must have seen something on Seiji's face because he laughed and blushed just a little. "I didn't want to be distracted while we were studying."

Seiji heard the truth in that and also the lack of shame. He colored. "Do you flirt with all your students?"

"Just the attractive male ones." He left the vicinity of the door and gestured Seiji farther in.

"What makes you think I'm homosexual?" Seiji asked stiffly.

"Actually, I have no idea if you are or not. My body's just decided you're attractive."

He felt a powerful urge to tell Nicholas some of the truth. Though used to following his instincts, which usually told him to run and hide whenever anyone got too close, he admitted, "I'm gay." Then he added, because Nicholas needed to know, "I'm not sleeping with you." To distract himself from the intoxicating smell of Nicholas's arousal, because it was, in fact, making him uncomfortably hard, he asked, "Where's your roommate?"

"Gone for the summer."

Did you have sex with him? That was unfair, assuming Nicholas slept with everyone, but Seiji knew it rose from a place of defensiveness. He was feeling exposed. He tried to put his attention on what he was actually supposed to be doing there. "Where should we start?" Then, remembering, "You're not going to test me, are you?"

"I figured we would do that in a less antagonistic setting. We're going to start filling out flashcards, but only with the stuff you don't know."

"I'm glad I brought two packs of cards," Seiji muttered. Then he saw Nicholas was grinning at him. "What?"

"Even in your preparedness, you're pessimistic." He took Seiji's hands and led him to the bed. "Come over here for a minute." And when Seiji was sitting beside him: "Tell me what scares you about Werewelsh."

And here I thought you were going to seduce me. "It's so hard to pronounce. And spell. And remember which parts are past, present, and future."

"Don't borrow trouble," Nicholas murmured as he took Seiji's hands again and began massaging them with his thumbs. "You only have to learn present tense for most of the verbs you're introduced to. This is just a sampling of Werewelsh."

"I know," Seiji said, his attention split between worry and the magic Nicholas was working. "But if I'm ever going to understand other werewolves when they slip into Werewelsh, I'll need to understand everything."

Nicholas kicked off his shoes and then knee-walked across the bed until he was behind Seiji. He began massaging Seiji's shoulders. "That's true, but all you need for your degree as a tracker is one semester of Werewelsh. You can always study the rest of the language later."

"Mm." Seiji leaned back into the strong hands. "You're good at this."

"Thank you." Nicholas leaned forward and kissed the top of Seiji's head. "Part of it is experience. The rest is my telekinetic powers.

Seiji smiled just a little. "I thought those were only good for helping pregnant wolves deliver safely."

"Nope. We help keep mother and baby from

shifting during the full moon. We ease stressed muscles in males and females alike. And we can encourage arousal." Another kiss to the top of Seiji's head.

It's not my imagination. He is *hitting on me.* Seiji's crotch tightened pleasantly but he did his best to ignore it. "I may be gay, but I'm not interested." He winced at the lie, knowing it would be heard. "I shouldn't be interested," he amended.

"Why?"

This was, of course, the question that *would* come up, but Seiji found he wasn't ready for it. "Just because."

Nicholas resettled himself, straddling Seiji's narrow hips. His erection was quite obvious as it was pressed against Seiji's ass. "If it's because of your pack, you're away from them right now."

"Yes, but they always seem to know what I've done. It's not a psychic thing. They can smell the change in my chemistry."

"Is your alpha dedicated to the idea that sex equals marriage?"

"Not exactly." But he did believe that psychic wolves shouldn't have sex at all. Or, if they did, only with members of their own class. *Translation: even hitting on a straight wolf accidentally is a crime.*

Although, it was quite apparent that Nicholas wasn't straight. *And I can't go back. Or at least I don't want to. Most of the time, anyway.* Seiji frowned at his circular, confusing thoughts. *Why not enjoy this wolf's company? Nothing I do could make my situation any worse.*

"You're right," he said. "I'm away from them." And the moon goddess knew he could use the comfort. Being alone, without pack approval or friends' support, desperation was becoming a way of life. He reached up, touching one of Nicholas's hands. "Will you have sex with me?"

And, as an afterthought: "Do you mind if I'm on top?"

"You want to claim me?" Nicholas sounded delighted.

Seiji grinned. "Well, don't play the blushing virgin or anything."

"I'm not good at playing what I haven't been in quite a while." But instead of resetting himself on the bed, Nicholas returned to the deep massage of Seiji's shoulders.

"I thought you wanted to get laid."

"I want you relaxed first. Do you mind if I use some of my telekinesis?"

"I thought you already were," Seiji admitted. "It feels wonderful."

"Is that a yes?"

"I guess… Oo…" Seiji let out a breath as warmth seemed to infuse all his muscles. "That feels…" He groaned in pleasure as all the knots released from his neck and shoulders. "You're good at this."

"Lots of practice."

Did that mean he'd slept with lots of other people? Seiji tried to care and found that he couldn't, at least not right then. He felt too good. And werewolves, like most magical creatures, didn't carry sexually transmitted diseases in their bodily fluids. *Assuming we actually get past the muscle manipulation point.* He tried to be worried about the studying they weren't doing, but the truth was that he hadn't felt this relaxed in what might be years. It frankly hadn't occurred to him that he could partake of the massage his pack reserved for pregnant females.

He put his hands over his erection. It throbbed

through his jeans and he smirked. "Can you use the magic on yourself too?"

"Are you asking if I can relax my asshole?" Nicholas had left off rubbing Seiji's shoulders and was leaving little kisses at the place where shirt neck and skin met.

Seiji felt himself blush. "Maybe."

"I can. And if we were doing this the other way around, I could make yours relax instead. Just like I can rub yours without touching it."

Seiji gasped in surprised pleasure as what seemed to be an invisible hand closed around his cock within his jeans and began to stroke.

"So…" Nicholas practically purred. "Tell me something. Why do you dress in clothes two sizes too big?"

Seiji blurted, "It discourages the other male wolves." The pleasant stroking ceased and Nicholas cursed.

"Are you telling me you were dealing with unwanted advances and your alpha didn't do anything?"

"Well, I never told him," Seiji whispered, feeling bereft. "Please, I don't want to think about that. I just want to have sex with you. Can we table any more discussion until later?"

"I guess," Nicholas murmured, "as long as you're not afraid of me."

Seiji laughed, genuinely amused. "You? I could bench press you if it came to that."

"You're so sure of that, are you?" Nicholas asked, his teasing tone back. "I'm bigger than you. Taller and broader."

"Yes, but, well, I've developed more muscle than the average werewolf." He prayed Nicholas wouldn't ask why.

This time, his prayer was heard.

"All right, Mr. I'm-Stronger-Than-You. Let's see if you can put your cock where your mouth is, so to speak. Claim me." Nicholas nudged Seiji off the bed.

They stripped, and Seiji was pleased to receive a quite thorough looking over while he gave Nicholas the same. He loved what he saw. Nicholas was hairy in all the right places, including a little on his belly, which Seiji found absolutely adorable. His hair was blond, lightening as it marched toward his balls. He even had the suggestion of a beard, which Seiji loved even more than the belly hair. Nicholas was just a touch scruffy, and practically perfect in Seiji's eyes. He wasn't hung like a horse, but had a dick of average length and breadth. Seiji, who had never been taken, wondered how it would feel to have such a modest and well made cock up his ass.

For today, he didn't have to worry about that. He would be losing his virginity in what he considered to be the best way possible.

"You're not as hairy as I'm used to," Nicholas said, but he didn't sound disapproving. "It's a sexy change." He strode forward and palmed Seiji's testes without warning. "I like that we're about the same size, dick wise."

Seiji's balls tightened pleasurably. "If you keep doing that, I won't last." He gently removed Nicholas's hand from its place between his legs. "Do you have lube? Would you prefer condoms?"

"Not worried about condoms," Nicholas said. "Gotta wash my sheets today anyway. And as far as lube…" He turned away and fished in the pocket of his discarded jeans. "I always carry some with me."

Seiji blushed, thinking of all the other male

magical creatures Nicholas had probably been with. *I hope I'm not a disappointment to him.*

Nicholas presented the little bottle. "Are you shy about preparing me?"

Seiji felt himself blush harder. ""Why do you ask?"

"I'm pretty sure you're a virgin."

How could he make that pronouncement without coloring? "I am," Seiji admitted. "But as long as you tell me what to do, I'll be fine."

Nicholas settled himself on the bed. He was on all fours and his legs were spread. "Get up behind me."

Well, he's taking the "tell me what to do" literally. That's probably for the best. Seiji did as instructed. Then he sat back on his heels and poured a generous amount of the lubricant onto his first two fingers. "One at a time?"

"Two, please. I can relax my muscles more than most, and if I get too much pleasure out of what you're doing, I'll come without you."

Seiji bit his lip. Then he inserted both fingers into Nicholas's asshole. It felt surpassingly odd, the heat around his digits. But in spite of the slight unreality of the situation, it also felt right. His cock twitched and an unexpected shock of pleasure bloomed in his belly as he scissored his fingers to widen his way.

Nicholas groaned. "A little to the right." And, when Seiji obeyed, "Oh shit, that feels good. Add a third finger."

Seiji used more lube and pushed three fingers in.

"All right," Nicholas said after a few minutes, "I'm ready. Make sure there's a lot of lube on your cock."

Seiji again followed instructions, wondering if

he'd used too much when it started to drip. *Well, he did say he's going to wash his sheets today.* He gripped his dick in one hand and laid his other hand on Nicholas's hip. "Are you ready?"

"Born ready, baby," was the enthusiastic answer.

Seiji slid just the head of his cock inside Nicholas and groaned as the muscles around him closed in. *That feels so good...*

"Keep going," Nicholas urged.

Seiji obeyed, and soon he was fully seated inside the other wolf. Unable to speak, he squeezed Nicholas's hip and hoped for a response.

"Yes," Nicholas panted, "You're good to go. Move."

Seiji did. The sensation was nothing like his own hand, or even like the invisible tightening of Nicholas's telekinetic power around his dick earlier. It was hotter, more slippery, and yet created more friction where he liked it. He groaned softly, mindful that they were in a dorm.

"Angle to the right."

He did, and Nicholas apparently had no trouble letting everyone know how he felt. Then Nicholas moved back against him and they were rocking together, pushing and pulling as one. Seiji's eyes crossed with need and lust and he thrust faster, deeper, and harder. Nicholas cried out, and his ass tightened more snugly than before.

He's coming. I made him come. That realization sent Seiji over the edge and he orgasmed into Nicholas's body. He all but collapsed on top of the other wolf as reaction flooded his nerves and muscles. He closed his eyes and rode out the last of the aftershock as his cock wilted with satiation.

He pulled out. Still unable to speak, he sat back

on his heels and braced himself on either side of Nicholas, leaning over him and smelling the intoxicating aroma of their mingled sex scents. Through his empathic link to the world, he felt Nicholas's intense satisfaction.

Then he felt the other wolf's attention shift, so he wasn't entirely surprised when Nicholas spoke. "Let's study now."

"Study?"

"Your Werewelsh. Now is the perfect time. Your defenses are down and you're relaxed." Nicholas rolled off the bed and grinned at Seiji. "We'll make flashcards and play strip with them."

"Huh?" Seiji fumbled his way off the bed. He realized he was blushing, mostly because of the innuendo that lived in Nicholas's emotions.

Nicholas handed him his oversized shirt. "Why are you suddenly shy?"

"Not shy. Embarrassed, I guess. And a little flattered. You want to have sex with me again even though we just finished."

Nicholas blinked. "How do you know that? It's true of course, but how do you know?"

"I'm an empath."

"Ah." Nicholas smirked. "Then you've known I wanted to jump you since our talk in the library."

Seiji knew he was blushing.

"Back to the flashcards. One. We get dressed. Two. We make flashcards. Three. Every time you get something right, you have to take off an article of clothing. Four. When you're naked, we have sex again."

Seiji laughed. "Honestly? And what if I don't get anything right?"

"Then we keep studying until you do. We should

probably keep meeting in my room since I don't have a roommate for the summer."

Seiji smirked. "I'm glad I found you as a teacher."

Nicholas grinned back. "I do know how to make things fun."

Seiji bit his lip, suddenly nervous. "You don't have any other Werewelsh students this summer, do you?"

"Nope. You're the only one."

Seiji relaxed. "Let's get dressed then, and make flashcards."

They began to put their clothes back on. Nicholas said, after a few moments, "You know, you're welcome to visit my pack whenever you want. I think they'd love you." He added, sounding a little shy, "We're the former Firos Pack."

Seiji gasped. "Your alpha was Firos William? The alpha above all alphas?"

"He was."

"Is it hard not to be the head pack in America anymore?"

"Not for me," Nicholas answered. "I was a wolfling when he was killed. I know it's hard for some of my packmates, like my parents. But I like Tilthos Charles. He's the one who made it so we don't have to follow the sex-equals-marriage tradition if we don't want to."

Seiji asked hesitantly, "Is Tilthos Charles your new alpha?"

"No. His name is Judah."

"Is Tilthos Charles..." Seiji dropped his voice. "Deformed?"

Nicholas snapped, "No!" Then he seemed to gain control of his temper. "Where did you hear that?"

"My alpha," Seiji admitted.

"He's a half werewolf. And he can't see very well. But he's powerful in other ways. He's defeated every alpha who's tried to challenge him for the right to lead our people. Including Judah."

Seiji could sense the fierce loyalty rolling off of Nicholas. "You really like the new alpha above all alphas."

"I do. He's LGBTQ, he's a scary good telepath, and he came into power not by fighting but because Firos William named him as his successor." He winked and some of the tension went out of the situation. "And he lets us have sex."

Seiji chuckled. "I'm glad of that." He finished tying his right shoe. "Now. Flashcards?"

"Let's do it."

Chapter Three

On June 11th, Nicholas saw the brightly colored poster. It was for the summer solstice dance in about ten days. It was advertised as a "mixer", and he grinned as he thought of all the different magical creatures who celebrated the longest day of the year for one reason or another. The Fae, both grand and common, rejoiced at the sun's ascendancy. Humans seemed to be indifferent to the holiday but nevertheless showed up at almost every dance, so they'd probably be at this one.

Werewolves were a little different. The summer solstice meant that the moon was visible in the sky for the shortest time during the whole year. In centuries past, this had been greeted with superstition and even sacrifices of different animals. Sometimes, humans had been killed in the name of appeasing the moon goddess. Nowadays, the longest day was greeted with a need to dance and sing, to dispel the maudlin spirits that could creep among even the most prosaic of wolves.

Last June, when he'd been a first year, Nicholas had gone to flirt. To see whom he could bring back to his bed. Now, all of his thoughts were for Seiji. What kind of party animal might the slight wolf make? Probably a good one, even if he didn't like to dance, because Nicholas just liked looking at him. And if the dance turned out to be too much for Seiji, Nicholas would go alone, enjoy himself, tease his cock mind, so to speak, and then go back to his room and bone Seiji.

With pleasant thoughts on his mind, Nicholas left the student union, leaped down the stairs, and jogged across campus toward his dorm. On the way, he passed several couples walking hand in hand, but he only specifically recognized Amaruq and his partner, New-something-something. As far as Nicholas was concerned, Amaruq was the best of those he'd never gotten a chance to enjoy in bed. Granted, Amaruq was a transgender wolf. That meant, in Amaruq's case, that he'd been born female. But Amaruq carried himself like a confident dude's dude and his boyfriend had better consider himself lucky to have scored such a catch.

He was almost past them when he thought of something. "Hey, Amaruq, c'mere for a minute."

Amaruq and his partner approached. Amaruq's eyebrows were up on his handsome, dark face.

"Do you know Seiji Watanabe, the first year who lives on the second floor?"

"That's *my* floor," Amaruq reminded him. "Of course, I know him." He grinned. "And I hear you're getting to know him pretty well yourself."

Nicholas smirked. Amaruq had never judged him for all the guys Nicholas had taken to his bed. "Do you think you could help him find something less… bulky… for the solstice dance?" Amaruq was known as quite the retiring but crafty fashionista. Rumor had it Amaruq blamed this on all the years his parents had tried to get him to embrace Western culture.

Amaruq frowned. "Well, Nootaikok and I aren't going to be here for that." He retreated a step or two.

Nootaikok took his lover's hand.

Amaruq, who had been smiling a little nervously, visibly relaxed. Apparently, Nootaikok was just what he needed.

"We're going to Alaska once my, uh, therapy thing gets finished." He looked down, obviously embarrassed.

Confused but single minded, Nicholas said,

"Never mind then. Have fun." But then his heart caught up with his mouth. He took in the way Nootaikok was hugging Amaruq with one arm and the way the slighter werewolf had shrunk against his boyfriend. "What therapy thing?"

Amaruq said softly, "Rape's a bitch."

Nicholas's hands were in fists and he was halfway to shifting before he even realized it. All he could hear was Seiji admitting: *It discourages the other male wolves.* Which, of course, implied that others needed discouraging. Granted, Seiji hadn't exactly said he'd been raped, but...

All of this went through Nicholas's head in the time it took to take two stalking steps toward Nootaikok. "You *scumbag*," he snarled.

Nootaikok put up his hands, palms out, and said, "I would never hurt my lover." Then he frowned. "You've seen us together. Does Amaruq look like I'm mistreating him?"

Nicholas thought about that. "No." He dropped his gaze. "I guess I just assumed..." He could hardly admit that since Seiji's pack had been harassing Seiji that he now found everyone suspect. That was illogical and completely driven by emotion.

Amaruq stepped between them. "Peace, Nicholas, peace. It was one of the grand Fae who broke in and held the second and third floors hostage back in February."

Nicholas backed off a little. "You're all right?"

"I'm getting there," Amaruq replied honestly. "No pregnancy, thank the goddess."

Nicholas felt his gut knot. He stepped forward and hugged Amaruq. "I'm sorry. I had no idea."

Amaruq squeezed hard and then stepped away. "It's not common knowledge. Keep it under your hat, okay?"

"I promise." He stood there, watching them walk on down the path, and thought, *He's a hero. To be able to survive that, still in pain or not... He's a fucking hero.*

He resumed his journey, traveling at a slower speed and with weight in his heart. When he knocked on Seiji's door about five minutes later, he'd mostly shaken the specter. And Seiji's genuine grin when he entered did a lot to erase the rest of it.

"We don't have a practice session until three," Seiji said. "And I have to leave for class in twenty minutes."

"News first, then a good fuck?" Nicholas suggested as he locked the door.

Seiji blushed. "Sure. What's the news?"

"The annual summer solstice dance is coming up." Nicholas watched in confusion as Seiji flinched and huddled into his overly large T-shirt. "What did I say?"

Seiji retreated to his bed and sat on it, hugging himself. Then he let go and straightened. "SearchLight isn't like my pack," he whispered. "SearchLight would never do anything like that."

"Like what?" Nicholas moved closer and touched Seiji's arm.

The dark haired werewolf didn't look directly at him when he answered. "In my home pack, we choose a member of the pack, usually an LGBTQ psychic wolf, to be kicked out of the pack for three days to appease the moon goddess. If that wolf survives for the three days, they're let back in."

"Survives?" Nicholas's gut twisted. "Are they hunted?"

Seiji nodded, looking miserable.

"And were you ever one of those?" He sat beside

Seiji and took his hands.

Seiji nodded.

"How did you survive? And how old were you?"

"Sixteen. And I made it because of a large patch of wolfsbane that grows about five miles south of our pack house. It's a great place to hide. That's where the one wolf who never returned probably hid."

Nicholas wanted to pursue that, a wolf who had dared to leave his or her pack and strike out on their own, but he needed one piece of information first. "What's your pack's title?"

Seiji opened his mouth. Then he shut it. He looked at Nicholas suspiciously. "Why?"

"Because my alpha needs to know about this. So he can tell the alpha above all alphas and get this fixed. Kicking a wolf out is bad enough, because if another pack found out, that lone wolf might be hunted. At least under the old laws. I don't know how Tilthos Charles does it now. But for your birth pack to hunt you after they're the ones who pushed you out? That's sick."

Seiji scowled. "You don't know anything about it. You're from a privileged pack."

He said that like it was a bad thing and Nicholas's hackles rose. "Hey, don't blame your pack's backward nature on me."

"I'm not telling you my pack's name. They are not backward and they are not barbarians or whatever else you might be thinking."

Nicholas had to admit he'd been thinking the word "barbarians" very hard, and apparently it had been forceful enough to make it into his emotions for an empath to pick up.

He stood and began to pace. "But this is wrong," he tried explaining. "The moon goddess doesn't need our sacrifices."

"How do you know what a goddess needs?"

Well, Seiji had him there. Unable to think of anything to say, Nicholas took out his phone and hit speed dial.

"What are you doing?"

"Letting my alpha know something's rotten in Denmark." The cell rang twice and then was picked up. "Alpha," Nicholas said at once, and he launched into a description of what Seiji had just told him. When he was done, he asked, "What can we do?"

Seiji snapped, "You can mind your own business."

"What does Seiji look like?" Mirla Judah asked.

"Japanese, I think, or Chinese. Black hair, anyway, and brown eyes that tilt up at the corners a little. He's short and slight --" *and sexy as hell* --"and he wears clothes that are too big for him."

"And he's standing right here." Seiji sounded furious.

Judah spoke directly to Seiji. "Please, young one, tell me what your alpha's name is."

Seiji scowled.

The power of alpha came through the phone then. "Tell me," Mirla Judah urged.

Seiji opened his mouth.

Nicholas felt the power too. He wanted to speak even though he had no idea what Seiji's alpha's title was.

Seiji shut his mouth, pressing his lips together firmly.

"Well, that's interesting. You're a strong dominant for one so young," Nicholas's alpha said. "I can't force you from so far away but I beg you to trust me. I won't let any harm befall you."

"You'd hurt my alpha," Seiji said.

"He's hurt you. He's not deserving of the title of alpha if he hurts his people."

"I'm not telling you," Seiji answered. "Not because I don't trust you, but because my alpha deserves my loyalty."

Nicholas could still feel the power of alpha in the air. It thrummed in his bones.

Maybe Seiji felt it too because he said, "If he hadn't stopped the others from harassing me once he finally noticed, I might tell you."

"What others? Members of your pack?"

Very quietly: "Yes."

"What were they doing?"

"During the dances, Frost Thaw and others, the male straight wolves would…"

"Tell me."

"Pretend I was female and grind against me." He glanced at Nicholas. "That's why I wear baggy clothes. It tempts them less."

"And your alpha put a stop to this?"

"Yes."

"You said they pretended you were female. Are the female wolves in your pack treated that poorly?"

Seiji covered his face with his hands. "I'm done talking."

"You won't tell who he is? Even though he turned you out to be hunted like a deer?" Nicholas asked.

Seiji shook his head. But then he dropped his hands and glared at the phone as if Mirla Judah could see him. "Why did you want to know what I look like?"

"There are only a handful of types of werewolf packs. Most are out of Europe, east and west, or

Britain. But there are four Asian-American packs, two from Africa, and one that I know of from Saudi Arabia."

Seiji looked nervous. "If you find out my alpha's name, what will you do?"

"Put you in touch with Tilthos Charles and let him talk to you." Mirla Judah paused and then said, "Nicholas, your intentions were pure, but you trod on the trust you have with Seiji. You should probably apologize." He hung up.

Feeling rebuffed, not to mention guilty, Nicholas glanced at Seiji. "I'm sorry," he said honestly. "I just can't stand it when I see someone in pain."

"I came to SearchLight to get away from my pack," Seiji admitted quietly. "But that doesn't mean I'm going to turn them in." He hugged himself again. "I'm not going to any solstice dance." He stood, squaring his shoulders resolutely. "I'll see you at three. I have class."

And he all but pushed Nicholas out the door.

Well, I fucked that up royally. Nicholas trudged his way back across campus, hating himself and feeling frustrated with Seiji too. Why wouldn't the wolf give up his abusive alpha? It didn't make any sense.

I guess I'll be going alone. And our easy sexual relationship is definitely at an end.

That hurt, but he told himself that was because he was having blue balls already.

Though his cock was quite flaccid.

* * *

The last two weeks had been awkward as hell for Seiji. Probably for Nicholas too, but Seiji kept telling himself not to care about the other wolf. Granted, dreams of Nicholas -- sexual and otherwise -- dogged his sleep, and he found himself thinking about the blond haired werewolf at odd moments during the day. Not to mention their occasional descent into teasing when they were studying together…

Oh, who was he kidding? He wanted their sex life back. But surely that was just his balls and cock expressing their opinion. He was getting further in Werewelsh than he ever would have thought possible, and maybe he could make that be enough for him.

Now it was the day of the summer solstice dance, however, and Seiji was brooding in his room.

Someone knocked on his door. He inhaled, hoping against hope that it would be Nicholas coming to ask him to the dance -- despite Seiji making it perfectly clear that he refused to see the other wolf outside of study sessions. But it wasn't Nicholas.

Seiji opened the door, prepared to tell whoever it was to go away. But when he saw that it was someone he didn't know, he was curious in spite of himself. "Hi," he said noncommittally.

"Hi. I'm Adam. Are you Seiji?"

"Yes."

Adam smiled uncertainly "Amaruq sent me. He said you needed to dress up for the dance tonight."

Confused, Seiji stepped back and Adam, naturally enough, moved into the room.

"I thought Amaruq and Nootaikok were gone to Alaska for the rest of the summer."

"They are. But Amaruq asked me to look in on you. He said you needed help finding something to wear." He shrugged. "You know how hard it is to say no to him."

That was certainly true. "How do you know him? You're not a student here, are you?" If this human was in fact attending the academy, Seiji had never noticed.

"I have a contract with SearchLight Academy to draw their students who can't be photographed." Adam shrugged, looking uncomfortable. "And I used to be Brett d' Reynard's boyfriend."

Seiji relaxed a little, although he was mystified. "What could I possibly have to wear?" He frowned. "I am *not* going to the summer solstice dance."

"Why not?" Adam raised a delicate eyebrow. He was taller than Seiji, but a little willowy.

"Because Nicholas will be there," Seiji blurted. Then he felt his cheeks grow hot. "Never mind. Forget I said that."

"Go in spite of him," Adam said firmly. "I'm going in spite of Brett."

Seiji hesitated. "Why did you break up with him?"

"I wish it had happened that way. We dated all through our senior year of high school and through our first year and a half here. But once he met his mother... He's been avoiding me." Adam shuffled his feet. "Rumor has it he's even dating a girl." He shook his head decisively. "So, fuck him. I'm going to find my own place in this world, with or without Brett."

Seiji sensed a welter of emotions behind those words and knew Adam felt a lot more pain than he was letting show. But courage and determination counted for a lot in Seiji's mind, so he didn't address it. And as he considered Adam's bravery, he found himself wondering if maybe he could go to the dance after all. "I don't have anything more, uh, dance-like than what I'm wearing."

"Did another wolf give you all your clothes? Hand-me-downs can definitely suck."

Seiji blushed again. "Yeah," he lied. But then he remembered what SearchLight had been trying to instill in him since he joined last September, that the truth was infinitely more helpful. "No. I picked them out to... um, I don't want to talk about that."

Adam frowned. But then his face smoothed out and he said simply, "You can borrow out of Amaruq's closet."

Seiji liked Adam for not pushing him. He smiled his gratitude. "Amaruq gave you a key?"

"He's the generous sort. Come on. Let's get sexy."

Adam's cheer was infectious despite the emotions lying just under the surface. The human was determined to grasp life by the horns. Seiji decided he liked that. "Thank you."

About an hour later, they walked into the summer solstice dance side by side. Seiji had chosen, with difficulty, to show off his six pack and well defined calves in a muscle shirt and cut offs. He wore a borrowed chain around his neck and a leather bracelet on one wrist with a wolf's head stamped on it. He'd been surprised to find that Adam had bracelets with different images of magical creatures on each one. Dragons, stylized genies popping out of lamps, hydras, and even phoenix.

He glanced right at Adam and had to admit that if his head wasn't somewhere else, the human would be quite attractive. He had hair the color of sun ripened wheat and warm brown eyes. He was muscular, although without a six pack, and his shorts showed off his tight ass and well made thighs to good advantage. Seiji was put in mind of a country song where two people sang about sending revenge pictures to their exes and saying they weren't going home alone.

Maybe we could...

But when he caught sight of Nicholas, all his

wandering thoughts snapped to attention like a soldier being called out in front of his platoon. Nicholas put Adam to shame. He was wearing solid black, sprayed-on jeans and a sleeveless shirt. He also had a chain around his neck, although this one was a choker. His jeans cupped his beautiful ass perfectly and the shirt hugged each well defined inch of his torso. He wore motorcycle boots with buckles, which somehow elevated his outfit from good looking to outstanding.

He was dancing with someone else.

Forgetting all about Adam, Seiji strode over and tapped the unknown student on the shoulder. "Excuse me, but that's my date you're dancing with."

He caught the surprised look on Nicholas's face in passing, but he had eyes only for the interloper. Not much taller than Seiji, he resembled a stocky tree.

The student dancing with his Nicholas scowled. "I don't see your name on him anywhere."

Seiji darted a glance at Nicholas, saw he was wearing a pendant on his choker, that it was a wolf, and smiled sweetly at the invader. "See that wolf?" He held up his bracelet. "I have the matching one." Thankfully, they did match, in color and almost exactly in posture.

Nicholas grinned. He looked both smug and flattered. "I didn't think Seiji would be coming tonight or I wouldn't have gotten your hopes up, Brett."

This was Adam's almost-boyfriend? Seiji wondered what Adam possibly saw in the magical creature. "You don't deserve Adam."

Then Brett showed he had a scrap of decency, or maybe just some self possession and dignity, because he shrugged, said "Well, I tried," and walked off.

Then they were face-to-face. Nicholas's eyebrows were raised and he looked both amused and exasperated. "You're jealous."

Seiji blushed. "Maybe," he admitted. "I miss my tutor teaching me in his special way."

"Is that all you miss? The sex?"

Seiji fought with himself for a moment. "No."

"Dance with me?"

Seiji nodded and stepped into the circle of Nicholas's arms. The music wasn't at all what he was used to, being in a foreign language. "Is that Werewelsh?" he asked in surprise.

"Yup. And it's very repetitive. Try to translate it."

With your arms around me? How am I supposed to concentrate?

He fumbled over the first few words and then came across a phrase repeated again and again. By its third iteration, he knew what it meant. "Love me, love me, all night long."

Nicholas grinned. "Keep going."

"It's a short night, but we'll make it long with loving hands and mouths." His cheeks burned. "Nothing like this will be on my tests."

"True." Nicholas sounded amused. "Keep going anyway."

But now it was all instrumental. Seiji laid his head against Nicholas's chest and just breathed in the other's scent, giving in to what he'd been longing to do for a fortnight. "You're wearing cologne."

"I am. Do you like it?"

It was entirely different from the musk enhancing stuff worn by most of Seiji's people. "I do." He inhaled and was treated to the aroma of Nicholas's arousal. "You missed me too."

"Just possibly," the other wolf answered with a laugh. "Missed seeing you in a more personal capacity, let us say."

Seiji spanked Nicholas and was rewarded with another laugh.

* * *

Two hours later, both of them stiff below the waist, they tumbled into Nicholas's bed. Their time at the summer solstice dance had been filled with flirting and teasing, touching, discreet stroking, and laughter. Seiji had thought he was going to spontaneously combust before he finally got Nicholas's clothes off.

Nicholas was wearing a butt plug.

"You were hopeful tonight," Seiji said, trying to hide his disappointment. "You were looking for anyone to fill your bed."

"Not really," Nicholas answered. "I probably would have *let* anyone in, but the one I truly wanted is here right now."

Seiji grinned and felt like he needed to confess. "I've missed you."

Nicholas smirked. "Of course you did. Who else has such a tight ass?" He waggled the feature in Seiji's direction.

I want to remind him that he can't ask about my people, but... But not now, when he had Nicholas exactly where he wanted him. "Do you enjoy spanking?" He blushed to ask it, but needed the answer.

Nicholas grinned. "Absolutely." He climbed onto the bed, naked except for the wolf choker. "Although I mostly love spanking with hands, not with leather."

Seiji climbed onto the bed and sat back on his heels. He struck Nicholas's right ass cheek. Nicholas groaned.

Seiji's cock twitched and he stroked himself absently. Then he slapped the left cheek and moaned softly in response to Nicholas's all over shudder. Then he removed the butt plug.

"Please," Nicholas gasped, "fuck me. I need you."

Seiji was fully erect now. He used spit to coat his cock, and then realized he was skipping a step. "Do you need my fingers first?"

"No. I'm well stretched. Please, just take me."

Seiji was seated inside the other wolf in less than a minute. The tightness around his member made him dizzy with pleasure. He groaned, leaned forward, and nibbled gently on the bottom edge of Nicholas's shoulder blade. It was an awkward position and he couldn't keep it up for long, but Nicholas seemed to appreciate it because he said, "You can bite -- gently -- if you want."

"Can't reach," Seiji confessed. "I'm too damn short."

"I like your height."

Pleased, Seiji felt himself blush again. "Thank you." He began to thrust slowly in, seeking Nicholas's sweet spot. He found it by accident, on the third push, and concentrated on stroking it over and over again. He was overwhelmed by the flood of scent and the rush of Nicholas's emotions. He was projecting lust, of course, but also a sense of rightness and contentment. Apparently, he'd missed Seiji just as much.

The fire started building in his balls and lower belly. Seiji asked, his voice husky with need, "How close are you?"

"So close," Nicholas responded. "But don't stop. It feels heavenly."

Seiji braced himself on the mattress with his left hand. Then he cupped Nicholas's furry testicles. Rolling the sac in his palm, he asked, "And now?"

"Shit, keep doing that and I'm going to come."

Seiji kept it up even as he thrust, angling to stroke Nicholas's sweet spot. "And now?" He gasped as Nicholas's entrance constricted around his cock. He stopped rolling the other wolf's balls because he didn't want to crush them as his orgasm claimed him.

Nicholas came less than thirty seconds later, shouting his bliss, apparently not caring who heard.

Chapter Four

Seiji couldn't believe how much he'd missed Nicholas. Being with Nicholas must be what living with a trustworthy pack would be like. After they made love, they moved to Seiji's room -- partially because all of Seiji's notes were there. They'd resumed their games of sexually teasing each other while answering questions from flashcards and added another game, one where Seiji had to translate words from Werewelsh songs that Nicholas promised were popular. Not all of them were as sexual as the one from the dance, but many were. The rest seemed to be divided into two categories: holiday themed and missing-home themed.

They spent the rest of that day and into the late evening practicing in a way that didn't feel like work. Then they curled up together in Seiji's bed and went to sleep.

Around about one o'clock in the morning, Seiji's roommate, Kevin, came in. He was making every effort to be quiet, but Seiji was a light sleeper. It had, in point of fact, taken him awhile to get used to Nicholas's snores and he'd only dropped off an hour before. In the pack house where he'd grown up, there had often been unwanted advances in the night, mostly from wolves who just wanted to prove their dominance in the most invasive way possible. And although none of those had gone beyond groping before he got up and moved, Seiji had gotten used to sleeping lightly and removing himself from any situation. There had been many a night, especially during high summer, when he'd slept outside.

He'd sort of explained this to Nicholas, saying he didn't like to be touched sexually while he slept.

Nicholas, after grumbling more or less to himself that Seiji really should give up the name of his alpha, said Seiji could spoon him. Thus, there would be enough room for both of them on the narrow bed but Seiji would be in control of the situation. It was a little awkward, Seiji being so much shorter, until he found a good position. But once he had, it had felt like the most natural thing in the world. A swell of protectiveness had filled his heart and he'd wanted nothing more than to keep Nicholas with him always.

Now, Seiji opened his eyes and watched Kevin cross the room and move to his bed. The human undressed quickly and slipped under his covers. He didn't seem to know he was being watched.

Seiji closed his eyes and fell back to sleep. Beside him, Nicholas hadn't stirred.

He woke around seven with Nicholas nudging him gently. "Have to pee," the other wolf murmured.

Seiji slipped out of bed and they both went to the bathroom. When Seiji stepped back into the room, Nicholas behind him and hidden by the door, Kevin said, "Seiji, we need to talk."

Seiji blinked, surprised by Kevin's serious tone. He looked like a man who had something urgent on his mind. "What is it?"

"Not in front of him," Kevin said as Seiji stepped into the room and Nicholas followed.

Nicholas bristled. "What's your problem?"

"Settle," Seiji murmured affectionately. "I don't have a lot of secrets from Nicholas," he told Kevin. *And you and I aren't exactly good friends.* Though they weren't enemies either. Just roommates who didn't know each other well. "What is it?"

"Fine." Kevin, sitting on the edge of his bed in his boxers and T-shirt, folded his arms. "You need to know that he's been sleeping around basically since he got here. Last year," he added for emphasis. "He's slept with everything that twitches and has a penis. You're too nice a guy to be just another trick."

Seiji scowled. He didn't glance at Nicholas, not wanting to see the hurt or defensive look in his partner's eyes. "I know all about his past." Okay, so he didn't, but Kevin was human. He couldn't tell if Seiji was lying. Right?

"Do you know that he's slept with only a few people more than half a dozen times? He'll be dumping you soon."

"I'm an adult," he reminded the human. "I don't need or want your mothering."

"I'm trying to look out for you," Kevin said, sounding hurt.

Seiji reined in a temper he didn't realize had been showing. "I'm sorry," he said more neutrally. "But I need to be free to make my own decisions." Now he did glance at Nicholas, wanting to reassure him. "I'm..." What he'd been about to say died on his lips when he saw Nicholas's face.

"Yeah," Nicholas said softly, "I know I've been a man-ho. But... It's different now."

Kevin snorted. "Why? You're not going to play that old tired line that you've actually fallen in love, are you?"

"Not love," Nicholas said, "but... Shit, Seiji, I missed you when we were fighting. Just working as your tutor wasn't near enough to what I wanted."

That rang with truth.

Seiji took Nicholas's hand and kissed it. "I can't say I love you either," he told the werewolf. "And I'm still angry that you told your alpha about my business. But I missed your laughter and your hands and..." He shrugged. "I want you in my life." He hesitated, wondering if he should put a stipulation on their time together.

Nicholas seemed to know what he was going to say because he promised, "I won't sleep with anyone else while we're together, whether that's another month or another five hundred years." He broke into a sunny smile and added less seriously, "Why would I go chasing anyone else when I haven't ever had sex this good before?"

Seiji glanced at Kevin. "Okay?" he asked. Then he added, realizing how defensive he sounded, "I appreciate your concern. Thank you for caring enough that my sleeping with Nicholas bugs you."

Kevin nodded. "I guess I sort of think of you as a younger brother."

"You're only two months older than me," Seiji reminded him, smiling a little. "And you're new to all this magical creature stuff."

"Yeah, but werewolf or not, you're still innocent."

Seiji bit his lip. He didn't *feel* innocent, not after everything he'd been through under Issei Ryo's leadership. "I can take care of myself," he said quietly.

"I know." Kevin was silent for a moment, but then he added, "But you're without your pack for the first time in your life and I've learned that means a lot more to wolves than it does to most humans who leave their families behind. And even for us, being homesick sucks."

Seiji felt his skin prickle. He did *not* want to think about losing the protection of the pack. *I need to become a tracker. Only then will I be safe from other wolves.*

Maybe Nicholas sensed how he felt or read his body language because he squeezed Seiji's hand. "Are you okay?" he asked softly.

Seiji didn't lie but neither could he think of anything that wouldn't sound like sniveling. "No," he admitted, "but I don't want to talk about it. Let's go for a run or something."

* * *

During lunch, eaten in the dining hall with maybe three dozen other people doing the same around them, Nicholas held up his hand to interrupt Seiji. The slighter werewolf had been going through verbs, naming and defining them between bites of a large turkey sandwich.

Seiji raised an eyebrow. "That one's right," he said. "It means 'to walk.' Doesn't it?"

Nicholas nodded. "Yeah, but I need to apologize. It's been bugging me all morning. I shouldn't have butted in the way I did." He didn't actually feel guilty about this, but he hoped Seiji wouldn't pick up on that.

His prayers went unanswered as Seiji's eyebrows climbed and he said, "You're not actually sorry about that. But maybe what you mean is you didn't want to hurt me."

Nicholas sighed. "Yeah, that's more like it. But I don't want you to be mad at me anymore."

"I'm not," Seiji said, and Nicholas could hear the truth of his words. "But I won't be sharing anything else about my pack."

His discomfort was obvious. He needed to talk about something. Nicholas could see it in his eyes. "What if I promise not to comment or judge?"

Seiji glanced around. "We're not alone."

"Then let's go somewhere else." Nicholas reached across the table and took Seiji's hand. "You're in pain. Let me help."

Seiji bit his lip. "Only because I think I'm going

to actually bawl if I don't find some way to relieve a little of this."

So, even though they'd gone for a run around the campus earlier, they did so again, this time in human guise instead of wolf form. Nicholas moderated his speed so that Seiji could keep up, but he didn't have to slow down all that much.

"It's like this," Seiji said on their second lap. "I have hidden my sexuality and psychic talent my whole life. You probably already know this, but every once in a while an unlucky LGBTQ werewolf is born with his psychic talents switched on instead of developing them in puberty."

"Is that what happened to you?" Nicholas felt his stomach tighten. He'd heard stories about how such wolves were treated, especially in the days before Firos William had declared all wolves, straight or LGBTQ, equal. Similar things had happened to witches in Salem, or that was what he'd learned in his Human History class last semester.

Seiji shook his head. "No, but I knew I'd have psychic powers sooner or later because I knew I was attracted to male wolves by the time I was five. My parents tried to keep it hidden, teaching me how to shut my mouth and hide my feelings. Until Firos William's edict, it wasn't exactly easy to be psychic."

Nicholas nodded. "But my pack has always been more accepting than most. By the time I was born, there was no hierarchy of straight and LGBTQ wolves."

"You're really lucky," Seiji whispered.

Nicholas skidded to a stop and took Seiji's hands. He squeezed them lightly. "Tell me. What was it like in your pack?"

Seiji looked down at their joined hands. "It was a

nightmare," he said at last, and his voice broke. Then he pulled free of Nicholas and began to run again. But he glanced back at Nicholas, obviously wanting him to follow.

Nicholas caught up with him and they ran in silence for a little while.

"About a quarter century before I was born, there was a werewolf who had his abilities turned on when he came into the world. When he was about five or six, he started telling his parents and anyone who would listen that the beta of our pack was planning to murder Iss -- my alpha."

Nicholas filed that slip, Iss something, away for later analysis. He wasn't sure if he would share it with his own alpha, but he would think about it.

"The accusations turned out to be right," Seiji went on, "but by then the pup had been run off during a summer solstice celebration. He hid in the wolfsbane patch, probably almost died there, and was spirited away by a SearchLight agent who happened to be in the area. When he was still in the pack, he was given an English name as a mark of disgrace."

Nicholas's guts were in knots. "This is…" He bit his tongue. "Why do you continue to defend an alpha this cruel?" Then he winced. "I promised not to be judgmental."

Seiji actually smiled a tiny bit. "You're just being yourself. In any case, he -- and my pack -- are all I have."

"You should come visit my pack. We would welcome you with open arms."

"I would miss my parents," Seiji confessed. "They were always kind to me, looking after me and making sure I wasn't ostracized."

"Except for the time you were chosen to be the

scapegoat during summer solstice." Then Nicholas sighed. "That sounded harsher than I meant it. I'm sure your parents did all they could." He realized he could hear the lie in his own voice and amended, "I mean, they probably did, short of leaving the pack. Did they have other family there?"

Seiji nodded.

"Then I understand it a little better," Nicholas said honestly. "It's really hard to leave family. I've just been really blessed to have a supportive family and pack."

They ran in silence for a while. Then Seiji said, "I'd like to meet your pack."

Nicholas smiled. "Good." He would find a way to extract the name of Seiji's pack eventually, but that didn't have to happen now. Maybe he could even leave it to his alpha, or to Tilthos Charles, whose own pack house was only a little more than an hour from Mirla Judah's. For now, he would be comfortable with what Seiji had told him. Or at least he wouldn't bring it up, or tell Seiji how disgusted he was.

I will protect Seiji if at all possible. And since it sounds like he doesn't really have a pack to go back to, I'll make sure he can go to my *pack for protection.*

And, a corner of Nicholas's mind whispered, *if he's in my pack then I will have a chance to woo him properly.*

Nicholas dismissed those words. He didn't actually love Seiji, did he?

Chapter Five

It was mid July, and Seiji's progress in his Werewelsh class was startling to him. He wasn't an expert by any means, but thanks to Nicholas he was passing. More than passing -- flourishing, at least enough to be getting a solid, low B. His teacher, Professor Lepa, was frankly surprised and just as obviously delighted in Seiji's progress. When he learned who the tutor was, he'd spoken of Nicholas with high praise.

So, it was with a light heart that Seiji approached Nicholas's room. But he stopped several doors down, his nose filling with the scent of unfamiliar werewolves. Strictly speaking, two pups and an adult male who wasn't Nicholas. Though Nicholas was also there. Shy and a little nervous about meeting his lover's packmates -- who else could they be? -- Seiji seriously considered turning back the way he'd come.

But Nicholas's nose was just as sharp, apparently, because he stuck his head out his partially open dorm room door as if he'd known Seiji was there. "Come on in." He flashed Seiji a reassuring grin. "My siblings and father won't bite."

Caught and not wishing to appear impolite, Seiji entered the room. It was crowded, the three additional wolves making the room seem smaller. Their resemblance to Nicholas was unmistakable. Like Nicholas, they had blond hair. Like him, too, their eyes were bluish green. All of them, Seiji's lover included, had a few freckles. Werewolves were considered pups until they tuned thirteen. These two were probably five and seven or thereabouts. Nicholas's father looked not too much older than his son -- a gift of werewolf long life -- and had a full goatee and mustache.

Seiji realized he'd been staring and dropped his gaze.

"You've had this one longer," Nicholas's father said neutrally.

Nicholas responded candidly. "I promised Seiji I wouldn't sleep with anyone else while we're together."

Embarrassed, and yet pleased, Seiji raised his head. "I'm pleased to meet you, sir. My name is Seiji Watanabe."

"John will do just fine, Seiji," the older wolf returned. "These are my son and daughter, Nicodemus and Mariam." He stood and offered Seiji his hand.

Seiji took it, feeling dwarfed by the man even though he wasn't taller than Nicholas by more than two inches. It was awe, he realized after a moment. "You're a father three times over?" he marveled aloud. This was unusual for werewolves in general, but downright impossible by the standards of Seiji's pack. He was the last wolf to have been born to them.

"Four, actually," John answered, grinning with unabashed pride. "These three will have a little sister or brother in about a month and a half."

Seiji wasn't sure it was wise to count werewolves before they were born and survived their first shift from human to werewolf, but he kept his mouth shut on that score.

Nicholas put in, "I've been helping my mother since my powers settled at around eleven."

Seiji blinked, startled. "Your psychic talents came in early."

Nicholas nodded. "Yeah, I guess. It's just like puberty hitting different wolves at different times."

Overcome by curiosity, Seiji asked, "How are you helping your mother?"

"Telekinesis. I can ease the shift of mother and

fetus from human to wolf and back again. Out of the womb, too."

Seiji grimaced and muttered, "If some psychic wolves can do *that,* then why in the name of the moon goddess are any LGBTQ wolves treated as second class citizens?"

"They're not anymore," John said with authority, "and frankly, they never were in my pack." He frowned at Seiji. "Is that sort of nonsense still taking place in your home pack?"

Seiji flushed, unable to stop the reaction. He didn't answer.

"Who is your alpha?" John persisted.

"Don't try that," Nicholas said, putting his arm around Seiji's shoulders. "He's loyal to his pack and won't tell who they are." He hugged Seiji even closer and said, "I don't know if it's the right way to go, but I admire his commitment to his people."

Seiji heard the truth in that statement and put his arm around Nicholas's waist. He smiled up into the other wolf's eyes.

"You should come visit my pack when my mother's about to give birth," Nicholas said. "Watch me work my magic. It won't be happening until near the end of August

Seiji relaxed, safe in his lover's words and embrace. "After I pass my class. That'll work." He'd taken, at Nicholas's suggestion, to saying "after I pass my class" or "when I pass my class." Because, according to Nicholas, positive thinking went a long way to making a thing come true.

* * *

About a week after the visit from Nicholas's family, who had apparently only been there to just "say hi," Seiji woke in the middle of the night. His heart thundered in his chest and his palms were sweaty. All of him was sweaty. He lay in the bed he shared with Nicholas, shivering a little and trying to get his reaction under control before he woke up the other wolf.

He attempted to manage this miracle by berating himself. *Trackers aren't like this. If you're going to be a tracker someday, it won't be accomplished by losing your mind over a nightmare. Just a dream really. Something that has no basis in fact. And trackers do not lose control over visions and megrims.*

"Seiji?" A whisper in the darkness.

He huddled into himself and swore silently, trying even harder to force himself calm.

"Seiji…" Nicholas rolled over, nearly pushing Seiji off the bed. Now they were forehead to forehead. He wrapped and arm around Seiji's waist. "What is it?"

Seiji shook his head a little. "Nothing," he lied. "Nothing I want to talk about," he amended.

"Is it about class?"

Seiji almost laughed. Compared to what he was feeling now, class wasn't even a blip on the radar.

"Okay, not about class," Nicholas said, apparently picking up on Seiji's thoughts in a way that had nothing to do with the telepathy he didn't possess and everything to do with perceptiveness. "Tell me. Please?"

Seiji shook his head again.

Nicholas rubbed his back. "Just tell me a little something."

"Your pack is perfect."

Nicholas laughed. "Not at all."

"Compared to mine."

"No, just different."

Seiji called him on that fallacy. "You hate what my alpha does." He stared into the other wolf's bluish-green eyes. "And don't even think about pretending that's not how you feel."

"I do hate what he does to your people. Who are my people too, by the way, because we're all werewolves. If I was an alpha..." He shrugged. "But I'm not even close to one. All I can do is put your needs into the hands of my alpha and hope for change."

"I need to protect him," Seiji said quietly. "He would punish my parents if I didn't. Because they protected me, kept what I am hidden from the pack until it couldn't be disguised anymore."

"What happened?"

And because it was asked gently, softly, Seiji answered. "I told you about being young and being attracted to other males."

Nicholas nodded.

"But I couldn't keep my arousal from the pack. I always managed to hide my scent with cologne and other things of that nature, but when my alpha was suspicious, he took that option away from me. Then I was exposed. My parents pleaded with him and he gave permission for me to take one of three paths. Become a subordinate member of the pack --"

"Which is going against Tilthos Charles."

Seiji nodded. "I know. The second option was to join SearchLight and be removed from the pack roster once I'd graduated."

"Even though being a member of SearchLight doesn't have to mean that at all," Nicholas said. "Many of our pack work for SearchLight now that there's an office outside of Buffalo."

"That's why I have to be a tracker," Seiji said, amazed to find himself confessing this. "Because then no one can touch me."

"What do you actually want to be?"

Seiji opened his mouth to say he wanted to be a tracker but something in Nicholas's eyes stopped him. "I don't know," he whispered.

Nicholas hugged him. "That's not a crime. So… what's the third option?"

Seiji blinked, remembered what they'd been talking about, and sighed. "To become a lone wolf and be hunted out of hand."

Nicholas pulled him crushingly close.

It felt wonderful to be hugged so possessively.

"You're never going to take that option, even if by some black miracle you are asked to leave SearchLight."

"If I flunk, you mean."

"You're not going to flunk," Nicholas said with authority. "But if that happened, again, by some black miracle, then you'd come live with my pack and you wouldn't be a lone wolf anymore."

As your mate. Seiji's heart leaped. Then he squashed the thought. *He's been sleeping around as long as he's been an adult. Maybe even earlier than that, for all I know. Once he gets bored with me, that'll be the end. Besides, he's been offering me a place in his pack for at least a month. Why did my stupid heart decide that means mating?*

Okay, so maybe his feelings were stemming from *Nicholas's* feelings because tenderness and devotion were pouring off the other wolf in waves. But those emotions did not have to equal mating. Surely Nicholas felt that way about his brother and sister.

Seiji got out of bed. "I don't think I can sleep anymore," he said truthfully. "I'm going to go take a shower and see if that will help me relax." He turned to Nicholas "Go back to sleep."

Nicholas rose and took Seiji's hands. "You don't have to," he said softly. "If what I said about joining my pack made you uncomfortable..."

"It's not that," Seiji answered. "I just can't think about my pack anymore."

"And being alone will keep you from doing that?"

"Well, no," Seiji admitted, "but maybe working the rest of the night will."

"You'll be tired for class."

"I know. But I can't justify keeping you awake."

"What if I want to be with you?"

Seiji kissed Nicholas's cheek. "I'll be back in the morning. I promise."

"I love you," Nicholas said.

Seiji gaped. He could hear the truth of what the other wolf said, but it still made no sense. "You think you love me," he corrected.

"No, I really do love you."

Seiji shook his head. "There's no way you can."

Nicholas scowled, and it completely changed his face. "Can't you hear the truth of what I'm saying? Can't you feel it? You're am empath."

Seiji backed away. "I feel it, but I think you're deluding yourself. What you love is my ass and my cock. That's all."

Nicholas's scowl deepened. "Fuck you," he snarled. "I'm giving you my heart here and all you can do is spit on it?"

"I'm not worthy of love," Seiji snapped. "Not when I need to protect a monster."

Thoroughly humiliated, he fled.

Chapter Six

Nicholas didn't sleep the rest of that night. Frustrated, furious, and definitely hurt, he went to the library and sought out the SearchLight archives. Seiji's denial of his feelings burned, but just as fiercely painful was the slighter wolf's confession that he felt unlovable.

Nicholas knew all about that, and as he crossed the campus with firm strides, he let the past take him for a few moments.

"You're no one's idea of good in bed," his first boyfriend had said. This was about two hours after Nicholas had turned eighteen. He and Christophe were a day apart, birthwise, and they'd abstained during the twenty-four hours between when Christophe turned eighteen and Nicholas did, although they'd had plenty of sex during their shared seventeenth year. This was coming out of left field.

"Why?" Nicholas had asked, his heart beating ponderously in his chest.

"Because screwing you is about as much fun as screwing a pillow." Christophe smirked. *"I've found someone better."*

Nicholas had gaped at him, just as, he thought now, Seiji had dropped his jaw when Nicholas announced his love. *"You can't mean that."*

"Why not? Because you're such a great lover?" Christophe laughed. *"Wise up, Nick."*

Pet names were a no-no in werewolf culture, a punishment or slur that couldn't be forgiven. So even though they'd grown up together, been lovers since they were seventeen, during a time in their lives when a year was like ten, Nicholas was furious. He punched Christophe, ending their relationship.

It'd cemented Nicholas into sleeping around, where he'd never get hurt but always do the hurting.

Yet here he was, in pain because of someone he'd slept with.

Reaching the library, he went up to the third floor where the private carrels and computers were housed. He jumped online at once. Getting the results he sort of wanted -- there were sixty-seven packs, both straight and eros, that SearchLight knew of -- he was disappointed to find that none of the packs were described as being from any particular nationality.

"All right," he muttered. "Fine. We'll do this the hard way." He knew in his heart that figuring out who Seiji's alpha was wouldn't solve his problems, but he desperately needed something to do.

First, he copied and pasted all the pack names into a word processing document. Then, he began patiently eliminating the ones he knew couldn't be Seiji's, starting with his pack, the Mirla pack, and Tilthos Charles's people. Then, he took out all the packs with names in Werewelsh or variants thereof.

An hour later, he was left with three names: Fehrna, which was led by a female werewolf, so that one didn't count. Two groups of people with names that he thought were Japanese. He jumped into an online translation program and looked up the first of the names.

He got "sun and rain" as that one's translation. That didn't eliminate it. He looked up the second, Issei. "All at once," the translation said. That didn't help either. Although hadn't Seiji said "Iss --" something once? When he was in the middle of spilling his guts in a way that'd given Nicholas hope for the future?

He looked up the location of the Issei pack and found it wasn't listed. Out of curiosity, he checked some of the other packs at random and found that they were traceable. What had this alpha done to make it so his pack couldn't be found by SearchLight?

But digging deeper only gave him the message "Classified by order of Tracker Central, Washington, DC branch."

He could still give the name to his alpha, but doing so now felt like a betrayal.

Well, Seiji betrayed me.

True, but maybe only by being honest. If he didn't love Nicholas…

"He never said he didn't love me," Nicholas whispered. "Only that he didn't think I could possibly love him."

He sighed. The realization didn't make him feel any better.

Even more frustrated, Nicholas shut down the computer and left the library. He paced the sleeping campus until dawn.

* * *

It had been a miserable two weeks. The only thing that kept Seiji going was his Werewelsh class. His focus had narrowed to passing, to the exclusion of all else. Including eating. He wasn't sleeping, and he wasn't talking to anyone, and he could barely put one foot in front of the other.

He'd lost his chance at a new home.

That had to be what was bothering him.

Oh, be honest with yourself, his deeper mind admonished him. *You miss Nicholas and you're feeling guilty as hell that you betrayed his trust.*

But he couldn't have loved me.

Why not?

Because no one does.

Hahaoya and Chichi do. He'd grown up calling his

parents the Japanese words for mother and father, and thinking of them in English was difficult.

He stopped walking on his way across campus to see the final scores from his Werewelsh class. He halted so suddenly that someone ran into him, told him to watch where he was going, and swerved around him.

Seiji watched the unknown student go with a bemused expression on his face. He hadn't thought to call his parents during all this mess. This, despite the fact that they alone had comforted him during all his years of misery.

He took his cell phone, which was actually his *chichi's* on loan, and found a bench where he could sit. He dialed his *hahaoya's* number.

"Seiji!"

The delight in her voice was impossible to mistake. *This is the simple joy I've missed by writing letters and email, rather than calling.* Seiji closed his eyes and allowed himself to savor her voice.

"How are you?" she asked in Japanese.

He hesitated.

"Seiji?"

"I'm confused," he admitted. "Do you have somewhere private we can talk?"

"Give me a moment."

Seiji listened to her speaking to someone, and then his *chichi's* voice joined hers. "Seiji, it's good to hear from you."

The simple words buoyed him up and Seiji felt like he did when they hugged him.

"One moment," his chichi said and there were sounds of rustling cloth and a closed door. Then the faint strains of a *tsuchibue*, roughly translated "clay flute," came through the connection.

"All right, my son," his chichi said in his mild, low voice. "What troubles you?"

Seiji hesitated again.

His *hahaoya* murmured, "You are safe here."

It was what she often said to him when he needed comfort and a place of sanctuary. He swallowed. Then he confessed all: how he'd met Nicholas, how Nicholas wanted to know their alpha's name so he could bring down the wrath of Tilthos Charles, and how Seiji didn't exactly know how he felt about Nicholas but that he cared for him deeply. And, finally, he shared how miserable he'd been for the last two weeks.

"I wonder," his chichi said softly, "if Tilthos Charles would punish our alpha or simply replace him. Though that is, of course, its own punishment."

"If Issei Ryo were free, he might come after you," Seiji whispered. "Or the rest of our family."

"It may be time for you to seek your own path. Away from us," his *hahaoya* said. "You're already on that path. You're at SearchLight. How are your classes going?"

Seiji bit his lip. "I don't know." Then he added, "I think pretty well. I'm almost certain I passed Werewelsh."

"Then you are safe in SearchLight." His *chichi's* relief was obvious.

His *hahaoya* murmured, "And you may have found love." Her voice was so soothing and soft that Seiji could have mistaken it for the wind.

"Chase him, this Nicholas of yours," Chichi urged. "But as you move toward a new future, never forget your roots."

Five minutes later, after hearing how his cousins were doing, Seiji hung up and resumed his journey.

Today his final exam results were to be posted. He went up to the classroom's hallway and sought out the message board. But before he was close enough to read the numbers, he saw Nicholas standing there, reading.

Seiji's heart cramped and he considered running away, but Nicholas proved he was still relying on his nose as he had the day Seiji approached his room, because he turned and their gazes locked. "I've missed you," came spilling out of Seiji's mouth.

Nicholas's severe expression softened a little. "It's going to take a lot more than that for me to let you back into my life." But then he caught Seiji's hand and pulled him to the message board. "Congratulations."

Seiji blinked, his eyes stinging with tears he refused to shed. He was sort of back in Nicholas's good graces, but not as far in as he'd hoped. Then he saw his final grade and let out a whoop. "Ninety-three!" He turned to Nicholas and kissed him full on the mouth. "Thank you for tutoring me."

Nicholas hugged him close. "Just for that?"

"No," Seiji admitted. "For helping me find my confidence."

He kissed Nicholas again, but this time he was aware that Nicholas wasn't kissing back.

He drew away a little and felt himself blush. "I have to do a lot of apologizing." He bit his lip and had to confess. "But I still don't think you love me like you think you do."

"It's been a long two weeks without you," Nicholas murmured. "Let's go talk about it in my room. And maybe you can still come visit my pack? If you want to."

"I'd like that." He heard the lie and winced. "I want to like it," he said honestly. "Can you promise your alpha won't try to drag my alpha's name out of me?"

"I can't, but I'll play referee if that helps."
It did.

Chapter Seven

About a week later, Seiji stood on the veranda of a gracefully built home that nevertheless held over sixty werewolves comfortably. He'd learned from Nicholas that the original house, the one Firos William had ruled for over a century and a half, had held too many memories for the remains of his pack to stay. The former Firos pack, now the Mirla pack, had moved to just outside Buffalo in one of its lesser known suburbs. Still close enough to the city for the longest commute to work to remain under a half hour.

There was a field out back of the house, a former farm the werewolves had turned into their own personal hunting ground. They chased squirrels and rabbits this close to the city, although the occasional deer wandered in and were enjoyed by all.

Seiji walked back into the house and used the mudroom to strip out of his clothes. He needed to run. Even though Mirla Judah hadn't interrogated him yet, Tilthos Charles was supposedly coming over for dinner and Seiji couldn't avoid his fear of the alpha above all alphas.

Naked, he shifted to his all black wolf form and went through the doggy door that was a little larger than most to accommodate werewolves. Inky black was a rare werewolf color, rarely found outside of Japanese werewolves, who tended to be either midnight in hue or blazing white. Despite his blond hair, for example, Nicholas's wolf was reddish brown, but Seiji was inky black from nose to tail, with two dark brown eyes that were the same color as those he possessed in human guise.

Seiji leaped down the stairs to the ground and headed for the far side of the field. He wasn't hungry, but he knew he would enjoy a good chase. He stood out against the bright green of the grass, but he didn't care. There was a band of trees separating this field from the next one and he made for those, meaning to lose himself in the shadows and the sweet smell of pine and oak and maple.

He was maybe a hundred paces from the trees when the wind shifted and he became aware that someone was following him. Someone unfamiliar. He scented the air, trying to learn more. Male, definitely, and also a werewolf. But beyond that, he knew nothing.

Unsure what to do, and wishing he'd had the evasiveness training trackers were supposed to get at the end of their second year under his belt, he sprinted for the trees. Maybe if he was lucky the wind would stay in his favor, blowing his stalker's scent to him and not the other way around. He heard the burble of a shallow creek and made for the water, hoping to confuse the other wolf more.

But soon, even as he waded in the ankle deep water, he knew he wasn't going to escape. The one following him was almost on top of him. Seiji, shivering, climbed out of the water and made for a clearing. He wanted to be able to see the threat approach.

When he arrived in the nearest open space, he set his back to a large rock and waited.

The werewolf that emerged from the trees at almost the same spot Seiji had left them was as inky black as Seiji himself. They could have been twins, although when Seiji looked into the other's eyes to judge their color, he was compelled to drop his gaze almost at once. This wolf was even more dominant than Seiji himself. He would have almost thought it was the alpha above all alphas if he didn't know that particular werewolf couldn't shift to four-footed guise.

The other wolf approached slowly. Then he did something amazing. He shifted to human and spoke. He, too, was Japanese, although there was no accent in his voice. "I won't hurt you unless you force me to."

Seiji hesitated. He didn't want to be caught naked in front of this threat. But if the other wolf decided they needed to talk rather than fight, he should take the opportunity.

He paused another moment, studying the slight, dark haired, dark eyed wolf in human guise. He was like so many of Seiji's people, short and yet muscular and powerful.

Deciding that to stall longer would be to invite trouble, Seiji shifted to human. He studied the other's collarbone since he couldn't meet his eyes.

"Seiji of the Issei pack," the wolf said, "why do you want to be a tracker?"

This was the last thing Seiji could have imagined. That the wolf knew who his alpha was… that made his stomach clench and his head swim with fear's lightheadedness.

"Truth now," the other said gently. "It must be so."

Feeling lost, and fearing that if he lied he'd be rent limb from limb, Seiji answered, "I want to have the power to kill alphas like mine."

"That's not what trackers do."

"No," Seiji agreed, "but if he somehow snapped and attacked humans…"

"You're thinking of falsifying evidence and having an excuse to take him out."

Seiji blushed scarlet.

"SearchLight doesn't need dangerous wolves as

trackers. Besides, with that attitude you'll never pass the psychological evaluations."

"I already --"

"I should have said the additional evaluations," responded the other wolf.

"I have to be a tracker," Seiji burst out. "If I'm not, they'll kill me out of hand."

"Your pack promised to make you a lone wolf, free for the hunt, if you didn't become a tracker?"

"If I ever left SearchLight's protection. And that means either being a tracker or never stepping outside of a SearchLight compound."

"There are fighters in SearchLight who aren't trackers."

"Yeah," Seiji scoffed, "but only trackers are feared."

He saw the blurred shape leap through the air behind the unknown wolf and didn't bother to warn him.

The new wolf was Nicholas. Seiji had smelled him coming although he had kept his face expressionless. Now Nicholas leaped upon the unsuspecting wolf with a basso profundo snarl.

The "unsuspecting" wolf threw Nicholas like he weighed no more than a rag doll. Then he stalked toward Nicholas, who was on the ground and shaking his head.

Seiji rushed forward, planting himself between the unknown and his lover. "Stop," he ordered, trying, and failing, to meet the other wolf's eyes.

Nicholas pushed himself to his feet and growled.

"Protective, aren't you?" The strange wolf sounded amused. "Nicholas, you know me. And you know better than to sneak up on a tracker."

Seiji gaped. "You're a..." He grabbed the scruff

of Nicholas's neck without looking. Nicholas was a fool to attack a tracker. And... This unknown said Nicholas knew him? "Please don't hurt him."

Nicholas shifted to human. He put his arms protectively around Seiji from behind. "Ethan, I'm sorry, but I couldn't listen to you threatening my mate anymore."

This time, hearing the profession of love didn't scare him. It filled him with galvanizing power. He covered Nicholas's hands with his own and worked through what his mate -- his *mate* -- had just said. "Ethan. But you're Japanese. Like me. Why do you have an English..."

Then he got it and his mouth went dry. He coughed harshly. "You're...." he croaked. "You're... the wolf they kicked out. The one they gave an English name and kicked out. The one my alpha and his whole pack tried to kill."

"The one they would have succeeded in killing if I wasn't rescued by a tracker team," Ethan answered. "And that's how I knew you were a member of Issei Ryo's pack. May I guess your parents are Keiko and Ryuji?"

Seiji swayed on his feet. "How do you know that? Most of my pack is black when they turn into werewolves."

"Yes, but you smell like my parents. Our parents."

"They never said it was their son, my brother, who was condemned."

"Well, I'm technically Issei Ryo's son, but they raised me."

"Why?" Seiji couldn't imagine Issei Ryo, who had no pups of his own, giving up his only son.

"Because a precog that he trusted, which is

strange in and of itself, told him I would be a danger to him if he raised me. So we're not brothers in blood, but close enough."

"They never said…"

"Of course not," Ethan answered softly. "They couldn't bear the thought that you might also be condemned. But," he continued, "becoming a tracker in order to get revenge is not the way to go."

"But without them being afraid of me…"

"You'll be under my protection. And the protection of my alpha, assuming we can find a way to temper your rage."

Nicholas hugged Seiji close. "He'll have my protection, no matter what."

Ethan nodded. "That's as it should be. But, no offense, Nicholas, Issei Ryo won't hesitate to kill two wolves instead of just one."

"How can you help?" Nicholas asked. "They already tried to kill you once."

"I'm no longer six years old. I have the backing of my entire pack. And," he added, smiling ironically, "I *am* a tracker. While that doesn't mean I can go around dispensing justice as I see fit, it does mean I have the backing of my tracker partner. Not to mention, because I'm a member of the Tilthos pack, I can call on the strength of the alpha above all alphas." He seemed to consider Seiji for a moment. "You need the tempering SearchLight can provide. I suggest counseling. It did wonders for me."

And without another word, he shifted back to his wolf guise and melted away into the trees.

Shaken and stunned, Seiji turned in the circle of Nicholas's arms. "That was my brother," he whispered.

Nicholas rubbed his back. He looked as floored

as Seiji felt.

Seiji rested his cheek against Nicholas's chest. "Am I really your mate?"

"If you want to be."

Seiji kissed him fervently. "Oh, I want. I want."

"Right here?" Nicholas asked.

Seiji grinned. "Right now," he confirmed.

They tumbled into the grass, naked as they were, kissing. They played over each other's skin, nibbling, licking, and even biting tenderly.

"Thank you for defending me," Seiji whispered as he slipped a wetted finger between Nicholas's ass cheeks. "Even though you're really stupid for attacking a tracker."

"I couldn't let him hurt you." Nicholas paused, groaning softly. "Does this mean you believe me?"

"That you're insane? Absolutely." Seiji added a second finger.

Nicholas huffed a laugh. Then he moaned. "Do that. Again."

Seiji pressed his fingers just where he had a moment ago and had the pleasure of hearing Nicholas swear.

"Do you believe that you are worthy of love?"

Seiji nodded, realized Nicholas couldn't see him, and said it aloud. "I have always been worthy. I needed your words and the words of my parents to believe it, but I have always been worthy" He paused before adding, his voice slightly unsteady, "I love you." He pulled his fingers out and covered his cock with spit. "I need you. Not just now but in my life. Always."

Nicholas whispered, "I need you too. You're my mate from this moment on."

They began to move together as Seiji claimed

more and more of Nicholas's body for his own. They rocked as one, groaned their pleasure as one, and shuddered in perfect counterpoint.

Seiji reached around and cupped Nicholas's balls, gasping when Nicholas's entrance tightened around his member. "Shit, that feels so damn good."

Nicholas bowed his head and growled, "Keep going. Fuck me. Hard."

Seiji rode him. They came, one right after the other, and collapsed in the grass.

When he could breathe again, Seiji asked, "So? When do you present me to your pack?"

"*Our* pack," Nicholas answered. "How fast can you become a wolf again and follow me home?"

Emily Carrington

Emily Carrington is a multipublished author of male/male and transgender erotica. Seeking a world made of equality, she created SearchLight to live out her dreams. But even SearchLight has its problems, and Emily is looking forward to working all of these out with a host of characters from dragons and genies to psychic vampires.

Series in the Searchlight Multiverse
A Pack of His Own
Three Brothers Fair
Dragon Schooled
Wolf Schooled
Dragon in Training
Fae Schooled
Lady Troubles
Para Schooled

Find more books by Emily Carrington at changelingpress.com/emily-carrington-a-207

Changeling Press E-Books

More Sci-Fi, Fantasy, Paranormal, and BDSM adventures available in e-book format for immediate download at ChangelingPress.com -- Werewolves, Vampires, Dragons, Shapeshifters and more -- Erotic Tales from the edge of your imagination.

What are E-Books?

E-books, or electronic books, are books designed to be read in digital format -- on your desktop or laptop computer, notebook, tablet, Smart Phone, or any electronic e-book reader.

Where can I get Changeling Press E-Books?

Changeling Press e-books are available at ChangelingPress.com, Amazon, Apple Books, Barnes & Noble, and Kobo/Walmart.

Changeling Press, LLC

ChangelingPress.com